He saw her through the glass. He didn't know her—he'd never seen her before in his life—but as their eyes connected, Luca's heart began to pound.

She was beautiful. Utterly gorgeous. Her wide lavender eyes had caught his attention first, and below them a generous mouth, slightly parted, was just begging to be kissed. Her sweater clung lovingly to soft, rounded breasts with just a hint of cleavage to taunt him, but it was something else, something he couldn't define, something fierce and elemental and soul-deep that drew him to her, and he wanted her so much he could taste it.

If he had any sense, he'd keep on walking. He liked control—and there was something very uncontrolled about his reaction to her.

But he was in desperate need of a shot of caffeine, this was the best *caffè* in the area and the only free seat was at her table. So he went in and walked over to her. He'd just get a coffee and go. How hard could it be?

'*Signorina?*'

She looked up, and her breath jammed in her lungs. It was the man, standing beside her, a crooked smile on those sexy, unbelievable lips, the dark, intense eyes that had locked with hers through the window glittering with something that if she'd had a shred of sense left would have sent her running, but she couldn't move. Even her lungs had stopped working.

'Are you expecting anyone to join you, or may I take this seat?' His voice was soft, Italian accent, and it trailed lover, bringing everything scr

D0550911

Mills & Boon® Medical™ Romance introduces you to

BILLIONAIRE DOCTORS

Hot, jet-set docs at the top of their game—
professionally…and personally!

These desirable doctors are international playboys—
Gorgeous Greeks, sexy sheikhs, irresistible Italians
and Australian tycoons.

Their playground might be the world
of the rich and famous but their
professional reputations are world renowned.

These billionaires dedicate themselves to saving lives
by day—and red-hot seduction by night…

Look out for more **Billionaire Doctors**
in Mills & Boon® Medical™ Romance,
coming in the next two months:

HOT-SHOT SURGEON, CINDERELLA BRIDE
by Alison Roberts—next month

SECRET SHEIKH, SECRET BABY
by Carol Marinelli

THE VALTIERI
MARRIAGE DEAL

BY
CAROLINE ANDERSON

MILLS & BOON

Pure reading pleasure™

**For Sarah, amazing font of knowledge
and maker of the best chocolate cake in times of need, and for
Alastair, Rhea and Eleanor who introduced us to Italy. *Grazie!***

First published in Great Britain 2009
Harlequin Mills & Boon Limited,
Eton House, 18-24 Paradise Road, Richmond, Surrey TW9 1SR

© Caroline Anderson 2009

ISBN: 978 0 263 86853 1

Set in Times Roman 10½ on 12¾ pt
03-0709-50422

Printed and bound in Spain
by Litografia Rosés, S.A., Barcelona

THE VALTIERI
MARRIAGE DEAL

Caroline Anderson has the mind of a butterfly. She's been a nurse, a secretary, a teacher, run her own soft-furnishing business, and now she's settled on writing. She says, 'I was looking for that elusive something. I finally realised it was variety, and now I have it in abundance. Every book brings new horizons and new friends, and in between books I have learned to be a juggler. My teacher husband John and I have two beautiful and talented daughters, Sarah and Hannah, umpteen pets, and several acres of Suffolk that nature tries to reclaim every time we turn our backs!' Caroline also writes for the Mills & Boon® Romance series.

Recent titles by the same author:

Medical™ Romance
A MUMMY FOR CHRISTMAS
THEIR MIRACLE BABY*
CHRISTMAS EVE BABY*
HIS VERY OWN WIFE AND CHILD†

Mills & Boon® Romance

TWO LITTLE MIRACLES
THE SINGLE MUM AND THE TYCOON
HIS PREGNANT HOUSEKEEPER
CARING FOR HIS BABY

*Brides of Penhally Bay
†The Audley mini-series

CHAPTER ONE

HE SAW HER through the glass.

He didn't know her—he'd never seen her before in his life—but as their eyes connected, Luca's heart began to pound.

She was beautiful. Utterly gorgeous. Her wide lavender eyes had caught his attention first, and below them a generous mouth, slightly parted, was just begging to be kissed. Her sweater clung lovingly to soft, rounded breasts with just a hint of cleavage to taunt him, but it was something else, something he couldn't define, something fierce and elemental and soul-deep that drew him to her, and he wanted her so much he could taste it.

If he had any sense, he'd keep on walking, because a woman like that just wasn't his style. He liked control—and there was something very uncontrolled about his reaction to her.

But he was in desperate need of a shot of caffeine, this was the best café in the area and the only free seat was at her table. So he went in and walked over to her. He'd just get a coffee and go. How hard could it be?

'*Signorina?*'

She looked up, and her breath jammed in her lungs. It

was the man, standing beside her, a crooked smile on those sexy, unbelievable lips, the dark, intense eyes that had locked with hers through the window glittering with something that if she'd had a shred of sense left would have sent her running, but she couldn't move. Even her lungs had stopped working.

'Are you expecting anyone to join you, or may I take this seat?' His voice was soft, gravelly, warmed by a rich Italian accent, and it trailed over her like the hand of a lover, bringing everything screaming back to life.

She sucked in a breath. 'No—no, I— Please, do.'

She gathered up the books she'd scattered all over the table— a guide to Florence, a phrase book that didn't seem to have any of the questions that she wanted to ask, a couple of tourist information leaflets she'd picked up—and made room for him, and as he sat down, his knee brushed against hers and a hint of spicy citrus cologne drifted over her and made her shiver.

He moved his knee, shocked by the bolt of lightning that had shot through him at the fleeting contact. Hell, this was going to be harder than he'd imagined. He dredged about for something sane and innocuous to say, then his eyes lit on the books. 'Sightseeing?' he asked, disgusted at his corny line, and she gave a little chuckle, but an endearing sweep of colour touched her cheeks.

'Wow. Sherlock Holmes,' she said drily, but there was a teasing little smile playing at the edges of her mouth and he wanted to taste it.

He dragged his gaze back to her eyes. Although her voice was cool and controlled, something in those gorgeous lavender depths told him that the accidental brush of his leg against hers had affected her as much as him, and he felt a kick of something raw and elemental in his gut. His eyes returned to her mouth, and he felt his mouth curve in response to her smile.

'Well, the English-Italian dictionary and the guide book were a bit of a giveaway,' he said, and decided it was time to introduce himself. He extended his hand. 'I'm Luca, by the way.'

'I'm Isabelle.' After a second's pause, she took his hand—only fleetingly, but it was enough. Their gazes locked, heat flared in her eyes and she sucked in a breath and pulled back her hand, to his regret.

Isabella, he thought, saying it in his head in Italian, tasting the word, feeling it surge straight to his groin.

'*Signore?*' the waitress said. 'What can I get you?'

A room...

He hauled himself back in line. 'Isabelle? May I buy you another coffee?'

'Oh—well, I wasn't—but actually, that would be lovely, thank you. Could I have a latte?'

'Sure.' He added a double espresso and a selection of pastries to the order, and turned back to her. 'So—what brings you to Florence, Isabelle? It's not the best time of year for sightseeing, in January.'

She gave a little shrug. 'I just wanted a break. It's so dreary in London in the winter, and I worked all over Christmas and New Year, so I thought I deserved a treat.'

'I should think so. Weren't you with your family?'

'No—my mother lives in Canada with her husband.'

'And your father? Brothers? Sisters?'

She looked slightly uncomfortable. 'I'm an only child, and I don't have a father.'

He frowned. 'I'm sorry.'

'Why should you be?'

Luca shrugged. 'Because my father is a very important person in my life, as are my mother and my brothers and sisters, and I can't imagine Christmas without them. So—why Firenze?'

It was her turn to shrug. 'I've always wanted to come here, so I thought, Why not? A couple of days—just time to take in a bit of culture, a bit of shopping, some lovely food…' She shrugged again and smiled. 'So here I am.'

'Alone?'

Was it so obvious? 'My friends wouldn't come,' she told him ruefully. 'They didn't mind the shopping, but they weren't interested in traipsing round in the cold looking at mouldy old paintings and statues covered in pigeon poo!'

Luca chuckled, sending shivers down her spine. 'And have you seen much yet?'

She shook her head, trying to drag her eyes off his mouth long enough to concentrate on what he was saying. He really had the most gorgeous mouth.

'Not enough. I only got here early yesterday, and I've done the Ponte Vecchio and the Pitti Palace and a couple of markets, but there's so much more to do today I don't know where to start.' And she was sick of sightseeing alone.

'Would you like a guide?'

She frowned, and for a moment he thought he'd pushed it too far, but then she smiled. 'Why would you want to do that?'

Because I want to spend time with you and I don't care if I have to trudge round every last damned artefact to do it?

He shrugged. 'I know the city inside out, and I can tell you what to see and what not to bother with. And my interview finished early, so I'm free for the rest of the day,' he added.

'Oh—didn't it go well?' she asked, thinking that it explained the rather beautiful suit and wondering what the interview had been for.

'No, it went very well—they offered me the job.'

'But not as a tour guide, I take it?' she suggested, fishing for more information about him, and he gave a deep, sexy chuckle.

'Me? No,' he said with a grin. 'I'm a doctor.'

'Oh!' she said, oddly relieved because doctors she understood. 'So—are you working in the hospital already?'

'No. I had the first interview there yesterday, and I had to go back today for another look round.'

'Interesting job?'

He shrugged. 'I suppose so. Wherever women are having babies the job's essentially the same, though, and I've worked there before, so it's perhaps a bit familiar—not enough of a challenge.'

She tipped her head on one side, fascinated by the coincidence. 'So—you're an obstetrician?'

'Yes—why? Don't tell me—you're pregnant.'

She chuckled. 'No, no chance of that, but I'm a midwife.'

'Really? Hospital or community?'

'Hospital—in the consultant unit, by choice, so I can make things better for women with high-risk pregnancies and try and give them a decent birth experience.'

A brow rose slightly. 'Are you saying that doctors don't?'

She smiled wryly. 'No—but their focus is on something different, and it's easy to get terrified by all the technology. My job's to take away some of the fear and uncertainty and give my mums the labour they want, and it's really rewarding—but that's probably all about to change, because the unit's being refurbished and I'm going to be sent off to some other hospital for months, so who knows what I'll be doing? Anyway, about you—is this a step up? Will you take it?'

'Maybe. But it's not just a career move, it's also a social move.'

'Back to the city of your misspent youth?' she asked teasingly, and he chuckled.

'Perhaps. Actually, since you obviously have an interest, there's something I'd love to show you that I wouldn't show just anybody. It's a bit gruesome but it's interesting. We'll start there, and we can do the mouldy paintings and the pigeon poo afterwards,' he said. 'That is, if you want to?'

She hesitated a second, then gave in. 'Well—since you're offering,' she said, wondering why a man so gorgeous would have nothing better to do all day but spend it with her.

But Luca didn't seem to have any trouble with that idea. He leant back so the waitress could set the tray down and smiled. 'Good. That's sorted. We'll have our coffee, and I'll show you the edited highlights of my city.'

So after they'd finished their coffee and demolished the pastries, he took her to the Museo di Storia della Scienza— the Science Museum—next to the Uffizi, and showed her a room where the walls were lined with fascinating but gruesome old wax models of obstetric complications.

'Oh, horrors!' she said, the professional side of her glad to be working in a modern, well-equipped hospital and her other side, the part that was a woman, just a little bit afraid.

'Now you see why the Italians invented the Caesarean section,' he said with a dry smile, and took her back out into the glorious but chilly winter sunshine. 'Right, the pretty stuff,' he said, heading for the Piazza della Signori by the Uffizi entrance.

Isabelle was awestruck by it all. The city was scattered with amazing and jaw-dropping sculptures in every piazza and public area, so that everywhere she turned she all but fell over another one, and they were all famous. 'It's like a Renaissance theme-park,' she said, making him laugh. 'It's incredible.'

'They're not all originals,' he pointed out. 'You need to see the original David—it's in the Galleria dell'Accademia.'

'Will we have time? We can't possibly see everything!'

'Of course not. I'm cherry-picking—showing you the best bits. Otherwise you'll just get overwhelmed.'

How true, she thought, but it wasn't only the art that was over-whelming, it was Luca, warm and funny and tactile, casually looping his arm around her shoulders to steer her in a different direction, resting his hand on her waist to usher her through doorways, his boyish grin at odds with those very grown-up eyes that were sending an altogether different message.

'Right. The Duomo,' he said after a lightning tour of the Uffizi, and led her through the narrow mediaeval streets to the magnificent cathedral with Brunelleschi's huge terracotta dome that dominated the skyline, then up all four hundred and sixty-three steps between the outer and inner skin of the dome and out onto a little walkway at the very top.

It took her breath away—especially when she glanced down over the curving dome towards the ground so far below.

'Don't look down, look out,' he said quickly, and moved closer to her—so close she could smell the spicy citrus of his aftershave and something else freed by the warmth of his body that made her ache to bury her face in his throat and breathe him in—and turning her with the pressure of his body, his other hand light on her arm, he pointed out the landmarks amongst the higgledy-piggledy terracotta roofs of all the buildings laid out below them.

A waste of time, because all she could feel and smell was him, all she could see was his hand, strong and steady, the long, square-tipped fingers and the light scatter of hair on the olive skin of his wrist tantalising her. What would it feel like to be touched by that hand, to feel it on her skin?

Stifling a whimper, she swayed, and his other arm circled her instantly and hooked her up tighter against him. 'Steady,' he murmured, but her heart just beat faster, because his body was rock-solid and very male, and she just wanted to turn in his arms and kiss him.

'OK?' he asked, and released her carefully, as if he wasn't sure if she'd fall over.

'I'm fine—it's just the height,' she lied, shocked at her reaction, and he slid his fingers through hers and held her hand firmly until they were back inside.

'Have we got time to see the real David?' she asked once they were safely back down, trying to concentrate and not squander the whole day like a lovestruck teenager, and he grinned.

'Feet not tired yet?'

She laughed. 'Don't be silly—I'm a midwife. I put a pedometer on one day and did over nineteen thousand steps. I can walk forever. How about you?'

'Ditto. I'm fine, let's do it,' he said. 'I'd love to show you and we've probably got time. You'll be blown away.'

She was. 'The anatomical detail's amazing,' she said, staring in awe at the statue—the real one, the one Michelangelo's hands had carved lovingly and incredibly skilfully five hundred years ago. 'It's so accurate!'

'Did you know he used to buy corpses and dissect them so

he could learn what happened under the skin? That's why his work is so lifelike—because it's based on real anatomical knowledge. Except the genitalia, of course,' he added softly in her ear, his grin mischievous. 'Pre-pubescent, so as not to shock the matrons and terrify the virgins.'

She suppressed a laugh, and they moved on, but the gallery was closing and they were turned out into the cold and dark of the January evening—and her wonderful day with him was over. She turned to him, hugely reluctant to let it end, needing to show her gratitude somehow.

'Luca, I've had the best day and I've taken so much of your time—would you let me buy you dinner?' she said softly. 'Just as a thank you?'

His mouth twitched. 'You're welcome to my time, *cara*—but I'll buy the dinner. I was going to suggest it anyway. Do you want to go back to your hotel and change?'

He'd agreed? Her heart soared and she beamed at him. 'Actually, I'm starving, so if I'm OK as I am…?'

He laughed softly, sending a delicious shiver down her spine. 'No, you're fine. Better than fine. Most of the women in my life would need at least two hours to get ready, and they'd never confess to hunger.'

'You obviously mix with the wrong sort of women,' she teased, and was surprised by the thoughtful look on his face.

'Maybe I do,' he murmured, and offered her his arm. 'Shall we go?'

She tucked her hand into the crook of his elbow and they turned into the wind, but the cold air struck her face and slid down her neck and she shivered and huddled down into her coat. 'Oh, that's icy. I didn't realise it would be so cold. I should have brought a scarf.'

'Here—have mine,' he said, and draped it round her neck.

'Oh—you'll get cold now!' she said, and then caught the scent of his body on the fine, soft wool and nearly moaned out loud.

'I'm sure I'll survive. It's not far to the place I want to take you, just round the corner.' And it was worth giving up his scarf just to watch her snuggle down inside it with that sensual sigh. 'Here, this is it.'

He opened the door and ushered her in, and the tempting aromas made her mouth water. They'd paused for a light lunch, but it and their coffee this morning were just a distant memory now, and she was more than ready, but it was heaving.

'It's too busy,' she said, disappointed, but Luca just shook his head and looked up, catching the eye of a man with a white apron wrapped around his ample middle, and he beamed and came over to them, arms extended.

'Luca! *Buona sera!*'

'*Buona sera,* Alfredo. *Come sta?*'

Isabelle listened to the warmly affectionate exchange but only caught the odd recognisable word, such as *bambini,* and then Luca switched to English. 'Alfredo, do you have a table?'

'*Si, si!* Of course, for you, my friend. Always.'

And with a bit of shuffling and rearranging, he fitted them in, dragging a table out of the corner and finding another chair.

They sat down, but because they were squeezed in, her leg was jammed against Luca's hard, muscular thigh. 'I'm sorry, I can't move out of your way,' she said, but he just smiled.

'Don't apologise!' he said softly, and she felt heat flood through her. Good grief, what on earth was happening to her? It was only a leg, and yet since the first touch of his knee against hers in the café this morning, every fleeting contact had been enough to send her heart into hyperdrive.

All day she'd been trying to forget it, but he'd made it impossible, constantly brushing into her, touching her—nothing in the least bit questionable, but it had kept her senses simmering all day, and then he'd offered her his arm and wrapped his scarf around her neck, still warm and heavy with the very male scent of his body, enclosing her in his essence, and the small amount of common sense she'd talked into herself had been wiped out in an instant. And now the heat of that solid, well-muscled leg against hers was setting it on fire and burning away the last fragments of reason.

'Relax, *bella*,' he murmured, his teasing eyes dancing. 'I won't eat you.'

Shame, she thought, and shut her eyes briefly at the images that leapt into her mind. Good heavens, this wasn't *like* her! She'd never felt like this, never reacted so violently, so completely to a man's touch.

But it wasn't just his touch, it was his presence, too. She'd felt him at the café before she'd seen him, felt his eyes through the window stroking over her like little fingers of fire. And now, every time he looked at her, there was something there, something hot and dangerous and unbelievably tempting. And she was totally out of her depth. It had been so long since she'd dated anyone she'd forgotten how to do it, and a bit of her wanted to stop the clock and breathe for a few minutes, just to settle everything down again and remind herself why she didn't do this.

But the clock didn't stop, and Alfredo was coming back, weaving between the tables, a bottle of Prosecco in one hand, two menus in the other, and he filled their glasses with a flourish. Luca lifted his and smiled at her. 'Welcome to Firenze, Isabelle.'

'Thank you.' She clinked her glass against his and sipped, the bubbles tickling the back of her throat as she met those hot, dark eyes. 'And thank you for bringing it to life for me. It was fabulous. Much more fun than trailing round alone.'

'My pleasure,' he murmured, his eyes locked on hers.

Oh, help. 'So—what should we eat?' she asked lightly, trying to break the tension, but it lingered for another second.

'The special's always good,' he said after a slight pause, and she dragged her mind back into order.

'Let's go for that, then,' she agreed, and tried to concentrate on the food, but she could hardly taste it. She was too conscious of the pressure of his leg against hers, the warmth in his eyes, the soft sound of his laughter wrapping round her and making her ache because it was so nearly over.

And then at last it came to an end; they'd finished their food, dragged their coffee out indefinitely, and their conversation had finally run dry. The day was officially done.

He set his napkin on the table and smiled wryly. 'Shall we make a move?' he suggested, and she felt a surge of regret.

He held out his hand to her, and after the tiniest hesitation, Isabelle put hers in it and stood up, desperately trying to ignore the sensation that raced up her arm. Her leg was still burning from the heat of his body, and when he'd stood up and moved away, she'd felt the loss of his warmth like an arctic blast. Crazy. He was just a man, just an ordinary man.

No. That was a lie, and she'd never been dishonest with herself. He was gorgeous—witty, intelligent, disarmingly frank, and his body, tall and powerfully built, with those midnight-dark eyes, made her go weak at the knees. His hair was slightly rumpled from the wind; she wanted to touch it, to thread her fingers through it and test the texture, and then draw her hand slowly over his jaw, letting the rasp of stubble graze her palm.

His lips, so firm, so full, made her ache to feel them. On her lips, but also on her cheeks, her eyelids, her throat, her breasts. Everywhere.

Relax, bella. *I won't eat you.*

Oh, lord! She looked away, dragging her eyes off him and bending to pick up her bag from the floor while she gathered her composure.

'I need the Ladies',' she said.

'Good idea, I'll meet you back here,' he said, and she made her way into the sanctuary of the quiet room with relief.

What was *happening* to her? She *never* reacted like this to men! Never in a million years. Or twenty-eight, more to the point. Over a quarter of a century, and no man had ever made her heart beat fast or her skin heat or her body ache with a longing so intense it almost frightened her.

But Luca did. Luca made her body sing with joy at the slightest touch, and when she rejoined him and he rested his hand lightly against her spine to usher her out into the street, she could have been naked the effect on her was so powerful. It was as if he'd touched her intimately, found her secret places and stroked them with the slow, sure hand of a lover.

And now she was being ridiculous! He was just killing time after his interview, indulging in a little mild flirtation, and she'd do well to remember it. It was nothing personal, he was just exercising his natural charm, and there was certainly nothing *intimate,* for heaven's sake! And even if there was, nothing was going to come of it. She was only here for one more night, flying out in less than eight hours! She'd never had a one-night stand in her life, and she wasn't starting now. But she wished there was more time…

'Where's your hotel?' he asked, and she told him.

'That's good, it's just near here.'

He tucked her hand into his arm again, his smile gleaming white against his olive skin in the darkness, and she caught the faint tang of his aftershave and that warm, male scent that was becoming so familiar—the scent that was also drifting up to her from the scarf, snuggled so softly and intimately against her skin, almost as if he was holding her.

She shivered, and he shot her a quick glance. 'OK?'

'I'm fine,' she lied, but she wasn't, because it was the end of their time together and she wasn't sure she'd survive if he simply took her back to her hotel and dropped her off, whatever her scruples, because for some reason this night— no, this man—was different, and if he asked her…

Luca paused outside the entrance, staring down thoughtfully into her eyes, and she reached up and kissed his cheek, her warm breath whispering over his skin and setting it alight. 'Thank you for the most lovely day. You've been so kind, Luca.'

He didn't feel kind. He felt on fire, more alive than he had in years, and extraordinary reluctant to let her go, but there was no way…

'What time's your flight tomorrow morning?'

'I have to be at the airport at five.'

He hesitated, not sure what was happening to him, just knowing he couldn't walk away. Not from this, because this— this was different, and he'd deal with the consequences later.

'It doesn't have to end here,' he said softly, and waited, his breath lodged in his throat, for her reply.

Isabelle's heart was pounding now, because this was something she didn't do. Never. She felt she was on the brink of a precipice—or at the gateway to a whole new era.

'I don't do this,' she said in a whisper, but he heard and he laughed under his breath.

'Nor do I.'

'I—I can't get involved.'

'That's OK.'

'So—just tonight?'

He nodded slowly. '*Si*. Just tonight, *cara*. If that's what you want.'

Why not? she thought. It had been years now. She was too fussy to sleep with anyone just for the sake of it, not desperate enough to settle for mediocrity, and she was alone by choice.

But Luca—Luca did something to her that no man had ever done. He made her heart race, her blood heat, her body throb with need. There was absolutely nothing mediocre about him.

If she walked away from him now, she'd never know what it would have been like to make love with the most interesting and attractive man she'd ever met in her life. A man she could so easily, under other circumstances, have come to love.

And maybe it was time to let herself live again—if only for one night. Taking her courage in both hands, she met his eyes. 'Your place or mine?' she asked.

He let out his breath in a rough, choppy sigh, then his lips twisted into a wry little smile. 'Yours is closer.'

Her heart nearly stopped, then started again with a vengeance as he took her hand and led her into the hotel. She picked up her key at the desk, her heart pounding, and they went up to her room in a taut, breathless silence, their fingers tightly meshed.

They'd hardly made it through the door before he reached for her, his mouth finding hers in a kiss she felt she'd been waiting for all her life. She dropped her bag on the floor, and somehow he peeled away her coat and his scarf that she was still wearing, and then his hands slid up and cradled her breasts and he gave a deep, guttural groan that turned her legs to jelly.

She whimpered, and as if it was what he'd been waiting for, he stripped the sweater off over her head, muttering incoherently as he pressed her back against the wall, his mouth on hers, his hands moulding her breasts again. His chest was heaving as she grabbed the front of his shirt and dragged it open, pinging buttons off in all directions and whimpering in frustration because she couldn't get it down over his shoulders with his arms bent and his hands doing such incredible things to her nipples.

She gave up with the shirt, her hands moving to his waistband, and then he dragged his mouth away and dropped his forehead against hers, his hands catching hers and stopping their frenzied fumbling. 'Wait,' he growled, his breath sawing in and out of his lungs. 'This is crazy. It's too fast.'

Crazy? Too fast? Maybe, but when he stepped away and released her, she felt a huge sense of loss. She didn't want to be away from him, not for a moment—but apparently that wasn't what he had in mind.

He stared at her, his eyes on fire, and shook his head slowly, his hand coming up to cradle her cheek with incredible tenderness, and she could feel that it was shaking. 'If we go on like this, it'll all be over in seconds,' he murmured roughly, 'and I don't want seconds, *Isabella*. I want hours. I want to take my time—savour every moment of this night. Touch you all over. Taste you.'

Her knees nearly buckled. *Relax,* bella. *I won't eat you.*

'Oh, Luca, please,' she whimpered, and he closed his eyes and muttered something that sounded halfway between an oath and a prayer.

'I need a shower first—come,' he said, pushing open the bathroom door and leading her in before turning on the water, then he held out his hands out to her and drew her closer.

Gentle now, and garment by garment, he slowly stripped away the rest of her clothes, his knuckles grazing softly over her skin. She closed her eyes, suddenly shy, but he touched her cheek, tipping her face up to his so she could see the heat in his eyes, so close to hers.

'You're beautiful, *cara,*' he said gruffly, his thumb dragging slowly over her lips. 'Don't be shy with me.'

She swallowed and flicked her tongue out to moisten her lips, and the tip caught his thumb. He paused, and she grew bolder, stroking it back and forth across the pad, then sucking it gently, nipping it between her teeth—just lightly, but it was enough to make him groan.

'You're going to drive me crazy,' he whispered unsteadily, and stepping back a fraction, he shed his clothes in record time then stepped into the shower, holding out his hand for her.

Her heart hammered against her ribs, and she let her eyes absorb him—the sheer potent masculine beauty of his body, so beautifully sculpted, so taut, so exquisite that he could have been one of Michelangelo's models—except this man would surely have shocked the matrons and terrified the virgins, she thought, stifling a bubble of slightly hysterical laughter, but the only thing that shocked and terrified her was her own reaction.

She wanted him—wanted to touch him—no, *needed* to

touch him, to feel him, test the texture of that hot, wet skin beneath her palms, and so she took his hand and followed him into the shower, under the streaming water that pounded over them like a tropical storm, and let her roaming fingers explore him, investigating the stark contrast between the rough texture of his body hair and the wet silk of his skin, following the streaming water from his shoulders, over his deep, solid chest to the arrow of hair that her downwards.

She moved lower, her fingers trailing over the taut muscles of his abdomen, and his teeth clenched and he sucked in his breath with a hiss.

'*Cara*, slowly,' he groaned, and, easing away from her, he squirted shower gel onto his hands and started to wash her, his hands firm and almost impersonal as they touched her everywhere. If it hadn't been for the blazing heat in his eyes she might have thought he was washing a child, but there was nothing of the nurturer in this man now, and when she filled her palms with shower gel and smoothed her hands over his body he gave a shuddering sigh, his breath hot against her face as he cupped her bottom and eased her against him. She felt the urgent pressure of his knee between her thighs and opened for him as his hand slid round and cradled the terrible, yearning ache that was building in her body.

'Luca?' she whispered, and as the water streamed over them his mouth found hers in a kiss so searing she thought she'd go up in flames. She felt the hot, sensual slide of his tongue, its probing so erotic, so explicit that she could scarcely breathe. And it wasn't just his mouth. His hand was moving against her, freeing a wanton woman she hadn't even known existed until this moment.

A woman who wanted him, this man she'd never met

before tonight but would have trusted with her soul, because already, in some obscure way, it belonged to him.

She felt fevered. She thought she'd die if she didn't have him, and then he hit the shower control, grabbed a towel and rubbed her roughly dry, then hauled it over his skin and threw it aside as he led her back into the bedroom.

His mouth found hers again, and then his thigh was between hers and he pressed her backwards until her legs hit the bed and he toppled her over, falling with her in a tangle of limbs into the centre of the mattress.

'Isabella,' he groaned, lifting his head to stare down at her, his hands shaking as they touched her. She was gorgeous. So beautiful. So perfect. So much woman. He wanted to go slowly but he couldn't. He needed her, and his control was in tatters.

Slowly, he told himself. *Slowly. Make it last.* He lifted a damp strand of hair from her face and pressed a tender, lingering kiss to her lips, then turned his attention to those soft, generous breasts, first one, then the other, kneading them gently and rolling her tightly budded nipples between his fingers until she whimpered and arched up to him, and then using his knee to ease her thighs apart, he turned his head and stared down at where the soft nest of curls hid her from his sight.

Dio, he wanted her. Wanted to taste her, to touch her, to bury himself inside her…

His mouth closed over one nipple as his hand sought her again, found the hot, sleek moisture of her delicate folds, felt the tremble in her body as his thumb found the swollen bud and stroked it gently, probing her warmth, testing her.

'Luca!' she sobbed, bucking under him, and he hushed her softly and moved on, his tongue taking over where his thumb had left off, and she cried out and trembled, her shaking fingers knotting in his hair. 'Oh, God, Luca, now, please!'

He couldn't wait any longer. He felt as if he'd been waiting for her all his life, and he couldn't wait any more. She was begging him, her voice cracking, and he moved over her, settling against her, feeling her body yield to him as he entered her with a long, slow thrust that nearly pushed him over the edge.

She gasped his name again, and he kissed her softly, trying to take it slowly, trying to give her time to adjust to him as he withdrew and thrust into her again, deeper this time, harder, bringing a tiny scream to her lips. He felt her hands clawing at him, her nails digging into his shoulders as she urged him on breathlessly, her body striving beneath him.

He needed no urging. He was on the brink, hanging on for her with the last shreds of his control, and then he couldn't wait any more.

'Now, *cara,* please, now,' he grated, his body shaking with desperate restraint, and then he felt the first contraction, the convulsions deep within her body closing around him and drawing him ever deeper, and locking his mouth to hers in a desperate kiss, he drove into her again and again, until the waves came up and claimed him and he followed her into the boiling maelstrom of their release.

She couldn't move.

He was sprawled across her, his head against her shoulder, his chest heaving, and she could feel the wild pounding of his heart gradually slowing until finally he lifted his head and stared down into her eyes.

'Oh, Isabella,' he whispered, and, wrapping her tenderly against his chest, he rolled onto his back, taking her with him so she lay draped across his body, her legs tangled with his, his hard, muscled thigh pressed against her tender flesh, still pulsing with the aftermath of the most incredible experience of her life.

She felt tears sting her eyes and blinked them away, but they still fell, and there was a stupid sob rising in her throat. She bit it down, but it escaped, and he tightened his arms and rocked her.

'Hush, *tesoro*. It's all right. I've got you.'

It was as if he knew how she felt, as if he felt it too, the amazing, incredible, tumultuous emotions that were cascading through her, and his hand stroked gently over her hair and soothed her, and gradually her limbs relaxed and she sank slowly into sleep.

Luca didn't sleep. The street light filtered through the shutters and brought with it disturbing and intrusive thoughts—thoughts that he dismissed for now. He'd deal with the consequences later. For now—for now he had Isabella, and nothing else mattered.

He turned his head and gazed wonderingly at the sleeping woman by his side. He'd never known it was possible to feel such a powerful storm of emotions. It was as if he'd come out of a coma. Everything felt—hell, it just *felt,* and so much *more* than it ever had.

He reached out a hand, then stopped before he touched her, because although he wanted her again, he also wanted to watch her, to lie there beside her and absorb her while she slept so peacefully at his side. And if he touched her, the fire would start again. He'd never known a fire like it, he thought, and he wondered how he could have felt so much for a woman he didn't know. Because he *didn't* know her. He knew hardly anything about her. She might be a real fruit-cake, a neurotic, clinging vine—or, worse, a money-grubbing little witch out for all she could get. He'd had it with that sort, big time.

But she wasn't any of those things. She was a good, decent woman who didn't do this. He knew that, from the straight-forward honesty of her response to him. He was just trying to talk himself out of something that scared the living daylights out of him, because if this was what it felt like, his life would never be the same again.

'Luca?'

He realised she was looking at him, and he put away his dark thoughts and dredged up a smile. 'Hi,' he murmured, and, leaning over, he brushed her lips with his. 'Did you sleep well?'

'Mmm. Fabulous. What about you? Are you OK?'

'Great. Fantastic,' he told her, realising that it was true. He felt better than he had for months—years—and it was all down to her. He kissed her again, then dropped his head against hers and sighed softly. She'd been so responsive, so passionate and tender and honest, and it had blown him away.

Made him forget all sorts of things he had no business for-getting—including one rather vital and critical thing that he just couldn't believe he'd overlooked.

He lifted his head and met her soft, sleep-hazed eyes. 'Mind if I ask you a personal question?'

'No,' she said slowly, as if she wasn't too sure.

'Are you, by a miracle, on the Pill?'

Isabelle's eyes widened, and she stared at him in conster-nation. She was—only to regulate her cycle, but it worked just the same. Which was as well, since she'd forgotten about contraception completely. Forgotten everything, even how to breathe at some points. And the Pill would only protect her from pregnancy. Oh, what an idiot.

'Yes, I am,' she said, and his eyes drifted shut, his relief obvious. He muttered something in Italian, then opened them again and grinned a little wryly, making her heart flutter.

'Sorry. I just—forgot about things like that, last night, which is crazy, because I never forget, but—it was amazing.' His voice softened and he reached out for her with his hand. 'You were amazing. Incredible.'

'So were you,' she said, feeling colour mount her cheeks and the now-familiar heat invade her body, but she ignored it, her brain, brought to its senses now, suddenly remembering all the other things she'd forgotten in addition to the pill she really must remember to take later on. 'Um—I don't really know how to say this, but—well, you don't need to worry about getting anything from me.'

'Oh, Isabella.' His fingers touched her cheek gently. 'Don't worry, you're safe, *cara*. I wouldn't do that to you.'

She felt a wave of relief, then common sense dawned again. 'Luca, what's the time?'

'Nearly four.'

No! She swallowed hard. 'I have to go soon.'

'I know. My car's not far away. I'll get it while you pack.'

He gave her a tender, lingering kiss, and then got out of bed. She watched as he pulled on his clothes—the shirt with no buttons, the crumpled suit, damp from the bathroom floor, and she wanted to cry. 'I'll see you outside in fifteen minutes,' he said, kissing her again, and closed the door softly.

He drove her to Pisa airport, and as they turned in he said, 'I'll park and come in with you—get a coffee or something.'

'No. I couldn't bear to say goodbye in public,' she said, wondering how she'd even do it in private, and so he pulled into the drop-off zone, cut the engine and turned to her, his eyes shadowed by the streetlights.

'Hey, don't look like that,' he murmured.

'I can't help it. I don't want it to end,' she said, unable to lie to him. 'It's been so special, Luca. Thank you.'

'Don't thank me—and it doesn't have to end,' he said softly, as if he'd read her mind, and she shrugged.

'Of course it does—and, anyway, we said just one night.'

'Can't I change your mind?'

She shook her head. 'It's silly getting involved. Long-distance relationships never work.' Relationships, full stop. And it might be better to let it go than to ruin the memories with reality. At least this way she could treasure them unsullied.

'There are ways,' he said, oddly reluctant to let her go without some means of contacting her. 'Tell me your number, *cara*. I'll call you when I'm next in London.'

She shook her head. 'No, Luca. That wasn't the deal—and I need to go now, or I'll miss my check-in.'

Oh, lord. She didn't want to go, whatever she'd said about long-distance relationships. She didn't want to leave him— couldn't bear to—and, crazily, she thought she was going to cry. She tried to smile, but her mouth wouldn't cooperate and she felt her eyes welling. 'Look—I have to go.'

'I know.'

He took her case from the boot and stood staring down at her, his eyes brooding and unreadable, and she flung her arms round him and hugged him, the tears welling once more. 'Thank you, again, Luca. Thank you for everything,' she said, and he shook his head.

'Hush, *cara,*' he murmured, and, lifting his hands, he cupped her cheek and brushed the tears from her face, then leaned in and touched his lips to hers.

It was a gentle kiss, tender and comforting, but then something shifted, and he threaded his fingers through her hair and anchored her head and kissed her with all the passion, all the incredible sensuality that he'd shown her last night.

Then finally he lifted his head, his breathing harsh, his face taut, but his fingers on her cheek were gentle. 'Give me your number—your address. I'll come and see you.'

'No—it's silly, Luca. We live too far apart—you're going to be working in Florence.'

'Maybe not. Isabelle—take my card. Call me, even if it's just to tell me you're home safe. Please. And if you change your mind…'

She hesitated, then took it and stuffed it into her pocket. 'Oh—your scarf!' she said, reaching for it, but he stilled her hands.

'Keep it. You'll be cold on the plane.'

She nodded, her eyes filling. 'Thank you.' She blinked away the tears. 'I have to go,' she said, choked. 'Goodbye, Luca.'

'Goodbye, *Isabella,*' he said softly, and his hand fell to his side, leaving her desolate. Grabbing her case, she ran into the airport without a backward glance before she made a fool of herself and started to cry again.

Luca watched her go, shocked at the emotion that ripped through him. He had to hold himself back, force himself not to follow her into the terminal and make her stay. He didn't know what had happened to him, but for some reason, everything felt different. Real. And he couldn't bear to let her go.

He waited until she was out of sight. Gave her time to come back, to call him.

Then he got back into his car and drove slowly out of the airport, his mind still full of the woman who'd blown his world apart...

CHAPTER TWO

HER JOURNEY WAS awful.

The flight was delayed, then they hit turbulence over the Alps and just about everyone was ill—including her—and by the time she got home she felt wrung out. She groped for her house keys, and found his card in her pocket where he'd tucked it as she was leaving him.

Luca Valtieri, she read, and a mobile number. She hadn't known his surname. It hadn't really mattered, not then. Not now, really. She wasn't going to see him again.

But she missed him.

Ridiculously so, with an ache that was almost physical.

Just a quick call, she promised herself—just long enough to hear his voice and tell him she was safe. And she could withhold her number so he wouldn't be able to call her back. That way she'd have control of the relationship—

No! It wasn't a relationship. She wouldn't let it be! But she was desperate to hear his voice, to have some kind of contact with the man who'd stolen her heart so suddenly.

So she rang him, and after a few moments she got his voicemail. She rang it again, just to hear his message, to hear the low rumble of his voice, the crisp message at odds with the man she'd spent last night with, and finally she spoke.

'Hi, Luca, it's Isabelle, I'm sorry I've missed you. I'm back. And thank you—for everything.'

Then she hung up, resisting the urge to give him her number. She could always call him again. Next week, perhaps. Or tomorrow.

No! Not tomorrow. Not next week, either. She was being ridiculous. She didn't want a relationship. Last time was enough for a lifetime.

She swallowed hard and then on impulse she turned on her computer and typed 'Luca Valtieri' into a search engine, expecting nothing, really, maybe a paper or two, some medical reference—and got a whole bunch of stuff.

Exstracts from articles in medical journals, research material, awards—but nothing personal, nothing to tell her more about the man himself except the fact that he was clearly very active and involved with his field of medicine, and he'd worked with a lot of English consultants whose names she recognised.

Silly her. She'd fallen—and how!—for a truly gorgeous man with a devastating smile and a kiss that had wiped out all the common sense she'd been born with, and not only that, he was funny and intelligent and dedicated. Thank God she'd refused to see him again. He was much too dangerous to her peace of mind but, oh, she missed him.

Oh, well. She'd get over it. She had before. It wasn't the first time her heart had been broken, although that time, of course, she'd been betrayed. Idly she wondered how she would have felt about Luca if she'd been able to trust him with her heart, but she couldn't turn the clock back and she had no idea how it would feel to have that much faith in a man.

Impossible. And if she'd allowed herself to fall for Luca, how much more would it have hurt when it all went wrong?

She swallowed hard. At least she'd had the sense to withhold her number, so he wouldn't be able to contact her.

And, besides, there wasn't time in her life to mope. Until her hospital's maternity unit refurb was completed she was working in another unit not nearly so easy to get to, so it was just as well Luca was out of her life because, frankly, with the extra travelling, she wouldn't have time for a relationship at the moment.

And if she told herself that often enough, maybe she'd believe it...

He'd missed her call.

He swore softly and dropped into a chair, resting his head in his hands. Damn. Of all the stupid, stupid things, to forget to put his phone on charge when he'd got back to the flat. But maybe...

He scrolled through to his incoming calls, and the hope died. 'Withheld. Damn.'

'Maybe she'll ring again,' his brother suggested.

He shook his head and swallowed hard. 'No—no, she won't. It doesn't matter. She didn't want to see me again anyway. I just wanted to—'

'Talk to her?' Gio finished softly for him when he broke off, and he nodded, his throat curiously tight. 'So are you going to go and find her?'

He shook his head. 'No. We agreed it was only for one night. I'll just have to live with it.' But hell, he didn't want to. He hadn't realised how much he was looking forward to speaking to her again—maybe talking her into letting him see her when he was back in London.

'So—what next?'

He let the air out of his lungs on a long, slow breath and met his brother's eyes. 'I don't know. Maybe I'll go back to London and finish off my research.'

'You could look her up—it's time you had a bit of fun. Where does she live?'

'Herne Hill, but I have no idea where or I'd go and try to talk her into seeing me again.'

'You must be slipping. It's not like you to have to chase after a woman. Did you disappoint her last night?'

He met his brother's mocking eyes with disgust. 'No, I did not—not that it's your damn business.'

Gio shrugged. 'So—what about the job? Mama will be disappointed if you go back to London. She was looking forward to having you closer to home.'

'She'd cope.'

'Of course—and who knows? You may even bring home a bride. Now, that *would* make her happy.'

He grunted and stifled the little leap in his chest that felt remarkably like hope. 'Unlikely. I have to convince her first—and, anyway, aren't you jumping the gun a bit? It was only one night.'

'Of course it was,' Gio said soothingly, and smiled. 'Just promise me one thing—let me draw up the pre-nup. And don't even contemplate getting hitched without one.'

He laughed. 'Relax, Gio. I'm not going to marry her. It's not on my agenda.'

'We'll see. Coffee?'

Luca gave his phone one last regretful look and slid it into his pocket. 'Why not?'

* * *

'What's going on?'

The group of women around the central nursing station didn't take their eyes off the office door.

'Richard Crossland's got someone with him. And he's a *hunk*,' her friend Sarah said in a stage whisper. 'He's been in there ages—they must be about to come out. I swear he's the most beautiful man I've ever seen.'

'Really.'

'Really. Really really really. Even you'd think so, Little Miss Fussy-Pants.'

Not fussy enough, apparently, or she wouldn't be moping about now with a broken heart six weeks down the line, Isabelle thought, and walked away towards the staff room to dump her bag. The Tube had been delayed and she didn't even have time for a cup of tea now. She certainly didn't have time to stand and ogle some stud who the girls thought was so damn marvelous.

There was a little commotion behind her, a sudden burst of activity that could only mean the office door had opened and they'd been caught staring. Well, serve them right, she thought, and glanced over her shoulder.

And stopped dead in her tracks.

'Luca?'

The word was soundless, hardly even a breath, but he turned his head and met her eyes, and the bottom dropped out of her world.

'Isabella.'

He crossed the ward in two strides, his warm hands cupping her shoulders, sending a shock wave through her body. She eased herself away from his grasp, horribly conscious of their rapt audience, her heart drumming against her ribs like a wild thing.

'What are you doing here?' she asked, choked by a flood of emotion that was threatening to unravel her.

'I could ask you the same thing. Your hospital's miles away.'

'Not nearly as far as Florence. Anyway, the unit's—'

'Shut for a refurb. I know that, you told me. They wouldn't tell me where you'd been relocated to, though. They were— well, let's say they were profoundly unhelpful. It didn't make it any easier to find you. So—how are you?'

She ignored that, her heart pounding as she took in his words. 'You were looking for me?'

'*Si*—for the last six weeks. I'd given up.'

Six weeks? Ever since…

'We weren't going to see each other again,' she pointed out, trying to sound composed while her heart was busy breaking all over again just at the sight of him.

'No. You didn't want me.' His mouth twisted into a wry smile, and her heart flip-flopped again and then contracted. Want him? She'd never stopped wanting him, not for a moment.

Whatever, it didn't alter the facts.

'It doesn't matter anyway, does it?' she said quietly, conscious of the stares of the other midwives still clustered round the nursing station with their mouths hanging open. 'What I want. I mean, you're here anyway, regardless of my feelings.'

'What?' He gave a startled cough of laughter and shook his head. 'Of course it matters. I'm not here to see you—I didn't know you worked here.'

'So why are you here?'

'I'm an old friend of Richard's. He heard I was back in London and asked me if I could help out. I owed him a favour—so I'm here. I swear, I had no idea you'd be here or I would have spoken to you first. Is it going to be a problem?'

She shook her head, feeling incredibly foolish and naïve. 'No. Of course not. Sorry, I misunderstood.' Of course he wasn't here for her. She was being ridiculous. Neurotic.

'So—why are you in London anyway?'

He smiled wryly. 'Finishing off some research—and I wanted to see you again if I could find you.'

No. She felt a flicker of panic. She didn't want this—didn't want to see him again. It was too much.

Her body was calling her a liar, and her heart was racing, but her mind was in panic mode and she shook her head and backed away.

'Luca, I can't talk about this here. I have to work.'

'So do I, now. But later—'

'No, Luca,' she said firmly, shaking her head and hanging on to the last shreds of her dignity. 'I told you I didn't want to see you again, and I meant it. I'm sorry, I don't want to talk to you, either now or later. Please—just leave me alone.'

'Isabelle, please, give me a few minutes—'

'No. Go away, Luca. Please.'

Turning on her heel, she ignored his protest, walked into the staff room, closed the door behind her and burst into tears.

'Izzie?'

'Go away, Sarah,' she mumbled, her hands pressed hard over her mouth to keep in the sobs that were tearing her apart.

'No. Oh, sweetheart, what's happened? Who is he? What did he say to you?'

She dragged herself together, sniffing hard and lifting her chin firmly. 'Nothing. Really—please—I'll be fine. I have to go to handover. I—I can't—'

'Rubbish. Here, you need a tissue and a cup of tea.'

'No. Well, yes, the tissue,' she said with a fractured laugh, 'but I haven't got time for tea. I've just got to get on.'

'So who is he?'

'Luca? He's a guy I met in Florence.'

Sarah's eyes widened. 'Really? Oh, my God—why ever did you come back?'

She laughed a little crazily. 'Because it was just one day? Because I have a life here, and he lives in Italy?'

'Well, it doesn't look like it. He's Richard's new locum, covering the maternity leave post.'

'What?' Shock nearly took the legs out from under her, and Sarah hugged her hard and steered her to a chair. 'Sarah, you're joking. He said he was doing Richard a favour, helping him out. I assumed he meant some research or something.'

Sarah shook her head. 'Sorry, Izzie, he's here, and he's working in the unit, and you're going to have to see him every day.'

'Every…' She dragged in a lungful of air. 'Oh, God, no! I'm going on holiday. How long's he here for?'

'I don't know. Weeks, I suppose. Months, maybe.'

Months?

'Will you be OK with that? Can you do it? Because I don't think you've got that much holiday,' Sarah said with a vain attempt at a smile.

Probably not, but—work with him? For *months?* Oh, lord. Maybe she could get a transfer? Or maybe she should just get a grip.

'Of course I can,' she lied, straightening her spine and blowing her nose hard. 'I'll have to. Just keep him away from me, and I'll be fine.'

And without giving Luca another thought—well, that was

a lie, but she had to pretend—she threw herself into her work. Which would have been fine, of course, if it hadn't been for the first labouring woman she checked.

Superficially, there was nothing wrong, but it was her third baby and third babies could often be a bit different. The notes contained no special warnings, the last ultrasound scan had been fine and there was technically nothing to worry about. Certainly nothing had been mentioned at handover, but the moment she went into the woman's room, she just felt a little tingle of suspicion.

'Hi, Julie, I'm Isabelle, I'm going to be looking after you now during your labour,' she said with a smile as she ran her eyes over her patient and skimmed the notes. 'How are you feeling?'

'Oh, I love the epidural,' she said with a heartfelt chuckle. 'It's marvellous. Just like going to the dentist, only I'm going to have a baby, not a filling!'

Isabelle smiled and checked her over, listening to the baby's heart with the foetal stethoscope. Was that a little hitch?

'Can I just turn you on your side, Julie? I can't quite hear.' She helped the woman adjust her position, checked again, then shook her head. 'I still can't hear enough. I'd like to put the monitor on you to get a better feel for what's going on.'

'Sure. It does seem awfully slow, this labour.'

'Well, that can be the epidural. Because you're lying down, you aren't getting any help from gravity, but I think it's just as well to check, don't you?'

She was setting up the machine as she worked, explaining to Julie how the cardiotocograph would give her the baby's heart rate and the pressure of the uterus, and also, most importantly, the correlation of the heart rate to the contractions.

And, sure enough, every time Julie had a contraction, the baby's heart rate dipped.

'So is there a problem?' she asked, looking more worried now.

'I'm not sure. Probably not, but it is dragging on a bit and I don't think your baby's very happy at the moment, so I'll get a doctor to take a look at you to be on the safe side,' she said with a reassuring smile. 'We might need to hurry things along a little.'

She stuck her head out of the door and looked around, just as Sarah came out of the sluice. 'You couldn't page the on-call register for me, could you? I've got a query with Mrs Marchant.'

'Sure—oh, there he is. Luca, Izzie wants you.'

Oh, perfect. Luca—of course, looking more gorgeous than a man had any right to look in shapeless scrubs. And Sarah's phrasing left a lot to be desired, as well! Oh, hell.

She straightened her shoulders and tried to find a professional face. She could do this. She could…

Luca walked towards her, wishing he hadn't taken this locum job to help his old friend out, wishing he'd just found Isabelle and spoken to her, but when he'd walked out of Richard's office this morning and seen her again, it had seemed like the answer to his prayers.

Now he wasn't at all sure. Ever since he'd set eyes on her again he'd been hoping that being forced to work together might give them a chance to get to know each other, find out if they had anything worth pursuing, but her face was closed, her lips pressed tightly together, and he realised that working with her could be a nightmare. She'd got issues of some sort. God knows what, but, given time, he was sure he'd be able to break through them. He had before—and how. He only hoped that he'd be able to remain professional until then, because all he wanted to do right now was wrap his arms around her and tell her it was all right—and if he tried it, she'd probably kill him. Thank God there was a patient in the way!

'Problems?' he mouthed as he reached her, and she nodded.

'Maybe,' she murmured quietly, and he realised with relief that she was going to behave as if nothing had happened—for now, at least. 'Julie Marchant, third pregnancy, straight-forward previous history, admitted late last night in early labour. She had an epidural at five a.m.—so that's three hours ago, she's had two top-ups, but progress has slowed right down even though she's virtually fully dilated, and there's a dipping foetal heart rate—nothing much, but I'm just…'

She ground to a halt with a little shrug and bit her lip, and he dragged his eyes off it and made himself concentrate.

'Is the head high?' he asked.

'A little. It's probably nothing, just the mother's position…'

But she looked troubled, and he knew better than to ignore a troubled midwife. He gave a terse nod. 'Give me ten seconds, I have to make a note of something and I'll be with you.'

Isabelle went back to her patient, and moments later he joined her, squirting gel onto his hands and rubbing it in as he smiled at their patient and tried to focus on her.

'Hi, Mrs Marchant, I'm Luca. May I call you Julie? Tell me, how are you feeling?' he asked, but as she talked and he probed gently with his questions, he was checking the CTG, watching their patient carefully, his eyes flicking to Isabelle's from time to time for confirmation of Julie's words.

And then, as much to hear her voice as for the information she'd give him, he said, 'Isabelle, could you run over the notes with me?'

Isabelle, she thought with a stupid tinge of regret, not *Isabella*, with that wonderful, slow roll of her name over his tongue, tasting every syllable. Damn. And she needed to concentrate.

So she filled him in again, showed him the charts and pointed out her concerns without alarming the patient, although there was nothing much to alarm her, anyway—nothing very untoward, nothing drastic, really, at all, and as she was telling him about it she thought, Oh, lord, he thinks I'm overreacting, because the baby's heart rate was only dropping a tiny bit—but…

'She's contracting,' she said, forgetting the charts for a moment, and he looked back at their patient with a smile that should have melted her bones, murmured, 'May I?' and laid his hands over her abdomen, the fingers of one splayed over the baby's head to feel for its descent, watching the monitor as the contraction progressed. This time, she was both pleased and concerned to see that the dip in heart rate was more noticeable. So she hadn't imagined it—and it *was* a worry.

He made a small, thoughtful sound and his eyes flicked to Isabelle's. 'She's fully dilated?'

'Yes, except for an anterior lip,' she told him, hoping that he was going to believe her and not give Julie an unnecessary internal examination, 'and she's been in established labour for four hours.' So the head should be lower, and coming down with every contraction, not staying stubbornly high as if something—the cord?—was preventing its descent.

'Hmm,' he said again, then looked back at Julie. 'I think your baby might be a bit of an acrobat,' he said with another of those smiles. 'The cord could be a bit tangled, and if that's the case, we need to untangle it for him. Unfortunately this means a C-section, but it's nothing to worry about and you have an epidural already, so you're all set. We'll take you up now, there's a theatre free. Is there anyone here with you?'

'No, my husband's taking the children to school and getting some food in. I was taking so long—oh, damn! Can we wait for him?'

He shook his head, busily disconnecting her from the machines and kicking the brakes off the bed. 'No, your baby's not comfy so I'm not happy to wait, but we'll look after you, you don't need to be afraid. Isabelle will stay with you. I'll get someone to contact your husband—do we have a mobile number for him?'

'Um—I think so.'

'OK. Don't worry, we'll deal with it. Isabelle, could you come to Theatre with Mrs Marchant?'

'Sure. I'll just hand over my other patients to Sarah—'

'She'll understand. Come on, let's go—we can't miss the theatre slot!' he said with a grin at their patient, but Isabelle picked up the hidden meaning and pulled the bed out from the wall, relieved not only for Julie but for herself that he'd taken her concern so seriously.

Sarah must have seen them go, because they were ready and waiting in Theatre, and Julie was on the table and draped in moments.

'OK, time to meet your baby,' he said the second he was scrubbed, and Isabelle ran in after him, her gown still trailing, and watched him do the fastest section she'd ever seen.

'Good call,' he murmured to Isabelle, clamping and cutting the cord which was wrapped several times round the baby's neck, and with a smile for the mother, he eased the tiny girl out and handed her instantly to the waiting neonatal team while Isabelle wondered what it was about him that his praise could mean quite so much to her. But then she stopped thinking about that, because the baby was silent, and in the normally noisy theatre they could have heard a pin drop.

'You have a beautiful little girl, Mrs Marchant,' Luca said in a calm voice, his eyes smiling. 'Well done.'

Julie's hand tightened on Isabelle's. 'Can I see her?'

'Not just yet,' Isabelle said, squeezing back reassuringly while her ears strained for a sound of life. 'They need to clear her airway.' Luca was still busy, but she could see that like all of them he was acutely aware of the deafening silence in the room, and his eyes kept flicking to the neonatal team.

'What's taking so long?' Mrs Marchant said, her eyes filled with tears. 'Why isn't she crying?'

'It only seems a long time,' Luca lied, but one eye was on the clock and it was ticking. One minute—two…

They were all holding their breath, because if they couldn't, then the baby couldn't—and then, when they had all but given up, there was a small, mewling cry, then a shuddering breath and a full-blown bellow of rage, and they all laughed with relief and carried on, because at that moment the sound of a baby crying was the sweetest sound in the world.

'Nice work, Mr Valtieri,' Isabelle murmured while Julie met her baby daughter, fairness making her give him his due, and his eyes met hers over the mask and softened in a smile that turned her heart to pulp.

'Ditto,' he said quietly. 'What made you get me when you did?'

She lifted a shoulder. 'Gut instinct?'

'I like your instincts, *cara,*' he said, and turned back to their patient, still smiling under his mask.

Maybe working with her would be OK after all—and given time…

* * *

'What time do you finish?'

She looked up from the notes she was writing at the nursing station in the centre of the ward and contemplated telling him it was none of his business, but apart from the fact that it would have been petty, it would take him ten seconds to check the rota.

'Nine-thirty,' she told him, and he frowned.

'So late?'

'I work a thirty-seven-and-a-half-hour week. So if I do three fourteen-hour days with an hour-and-a-half break, I've done my hours. And I get four days off.'

'But you haven't had a break yet.'

She met his scowl with a dry laugh. 'That's right. I usually don't.'

'But that's not good for you—and it's not fair.'

She couldn't disagree, so she just shrugged and carried on with her notes. Until a large hand arrived in the centre of the page, the fingers splayed across it so she couldn't see. The fingers which had touched her with so much skill, making her body sing...

'Come and have a coffee, at least. We need to talk.'

'I don't think so. I told you that earlier. We're working together, by an unhappy coincidence, but that's all. Our relationship is professional only, Mr Valtieri, and that's the way it's staying.'

'Has anyone ever told you you're stubborn?'

'It's one of my more endearing qualities—but it's nothing to do with being stubborn. I just don't like my wishes being ignored.'

'I didn't ignore them!'

'So what are you doing here?'

He closed his eyes, growling in frustration. 'It was coincidence, as you said.'

'You were looking for me,' she reminded him, and a flash of dark colour swept over his cheekbones.

'I had been. I just wanted a chance to see you.'

'Well, you should have checked if I wanted to see you before you wasted your time, Luca.'

'Maybe I should. Maybe I would have, if you'd given me your number, but this is nothing to do with that. This is just chance, and I'm sorry if you don't like it, *Isabella,* but since I'm here…'

Isabella. With at least two more syllables, and a rolling purr that made her heart hitch. Well, it wouldn't work. Her heart could hitch all it liked, but she wasn't going to let herself get drawn into a relationship with him by that flagrant Italian charm.

Except professionally, and only then because she had no choice. And she couldn't do that if she allowed him to creep under her guard.

He sighed. 'Isabella, we do need to talk about this,' he said quietly. 'Maybe not now, but soon. At the very least, you owe me the chance to—'

'I owe you nothing,' she said bluntly.

He leant over the desk so his face was mere inches from hers. 'Then at least do me the decency of hearing me out.'

Isabelle swallowed. He was so close that she could smell him, smell the combination of spice and citrus and man that had trashed her defences so thoroughly in Florence, so that even now the evocative scent brought it all back and left her weak and wanting.

She shut her eyes and stifled the whimper. 'Luca, I don't want to. You've come and found me, I didn't want to see you, that's the end of it.'

'Not for me.'

'Well, tough. It is for me, and it takes two. Go and talk to Richard if you want someone to talk to. I'm not opening myself up to hurt all over again just to give you closure.'

'All over again? Is that what this is about, some man who hurt you? Who was it, Isabelle? Who hurt you so much you're afraid to try again?'

She met his eyes in desperation. 'Luca! Go away!'

He sighed softly under his breath. 'OK—for now. But I'm not finished, and we need to do this somewhere a little more private.'

She contemplated saying no, but he wasn't going to give up, so she agreed, grudgingly. 'Oh, for God's sake, all right. I'll have coffee with you later, when I've finished this, but not now. Now, please move your hand,' she said calmly, although her heart was pounding, but as he opened his mouth to say something his pager bleeped.

He gave a low growl of frustration, muttered, 'Later—and don't forget,' and stalked off down the ward, muttering something in Italian.

'Oh, that man is so-o-o sexy!' one of the midwives murmured as she walked past, and Isabelle closed her eyes.

He might be sexy—she could testify to that—but she wasn't going to be influenced by it. She'd been stupid enough already and she wasn't letting him any further into her life. She completed the labour report she was writing up for Julie Marchant, slapped the file onto the heap and reached for the next one.

She'd hear him out, over coffee, as she'd agreed, but that was all. She wasn't going to let him get to her. No way.

CHAPTER THREE

'WHAT ARE YOU doing?'

'Taking you home.'

She turned up her coat collar against the February chill and sighed shortly. 'I thought we were going for coffee? I don't need to be taken home.'

'I disagree. It's dark, it's late and you've worked fifteen hours without a proper break. You can't go home alone and unaccompanied, especially not by the time we've had coffee, it's not safe.'

She glared at him in exasperation. 'Luca, I'm twenty-eight! I've lived in London all my life, and I've been doing this journey for weeks now. It's perfectly safe!'

'But it's a long way to Herne Hill—that is where you said you live, isn't it? Unless you've moved house, as well, during the refurb?'

She contemplated lying, but it went against the grain, and, anyway, he only had to check the HR files. Probably had already. 'No—no, I haven't moved house,' she told him, amazed that he'd remembered where she lived from her fleeting mention of it weeks ago, 'but the journey's perfectly straightforward.'

'Straightforward?'

She rolled her eyes. 'I walk to the Tube, get the train to Victoria, get the bus to the end of the road next to mine and walk home.'

'In the dark? That's *not* safe.'

'It's *perfectly* safe. There are lots of streetlights.' Although it wasn't great. There were too many trees shading the lights, and there were several dark spots where she often felt a little nervous, but there was no way on God's green earth she was telling Luca that.

'And how long does this whole *straightforward* journey take you?'

She shrugged. 'Forty-five minutes?'

He swore—in English, so she could understand this time, his accent heavier as he became frustrated with her—and went on, 'I'm taking you home. Get used to it.'

'Only if I tell you the address—which I have no intention of doing. It's bad enough that you know where I work.'

'Oh, for God's sake, Isabelle! If I wanted to know your address, I'd ask Human Resources,' he pointed out. 'I'm sure I could come up with some plausible reason for needing it.'

She was sure he could.

She gave up, frustrated to bits but too tired to argue any longer.

'All right,' she snapped, 'you can take me home, if your crazy Latin sense of honour demands it, but that's it. You're not coming in. I don't want this, Luca.'

His shoulders dropped, and he stabbed a hand through his hair and gave a tired sigh that pulled at her reluctant heart-strings. 'This? What this? I just want to talk to you, Isabelle. I *need* to talk to you.'

'Why? There's nothing to say.'

'Because I've been looking for you for weeks,' he said quietly, 'and now I've found you, by a miracle, I would appreciate a chance to talk to you—even if it's only so you can tell me to go to hell. You still owe me that coffee, since you managed to avoid taking a break all day.'

She hesitated, but he was right, she had promised, and she didn't go back on her word. 'OK,' she said flatly. 'You can take me home, if you absolutely have to, and you can have a coffee and get all this off your chest so you have closure, and then you can leave.'

'I don't want closure.'

'Well, it's all you're going to get, so take your pick.'

His smile was cynical. 'You're all heart, you know that?'

'Or maybe I'll just go home on the Tube on my own.'

She turned and walked off, and after a second she heard his firm, solid footfall behind her. And for some crazy, stupid reason, her heart did a happy little jiggle. She squashed the smile and kept walking, then she felt his hand on her arm.

'Isabelle, stop. I intend to take you home whether I drive you in my car or follow you on foot, so why don't you just choose the car and make it easier for both of us?'

'Some choice,' she grumbled, but in truth she was exhausted, and the very thought of walking to the Tube, sitting in the smelly, busy carriage with all the revellers out for the night, then waiting for a bus and walking for another ten minutes at the other end was too depressing to contemplate.

'Of course, if you come in my car, we have the heater, we won't get wet in the rain and I don't have to make the same ridiculous journey back. But it's up to you.'

Stupidly—because it was his idea to take her home and

nothing at all to do with what she wanted—she felt guilty at the thought of him having to make the return journey the hard way. After all, his day had been just as long as hers. And the car did sound *awfully* tempting. Then a dribble off the edge of the canopy ran down the back of her neck and made up her mind.

'Have it your way, then,' she said grudgingly, and immediately felt rude and ungrateful and mean. And she hated that, because she wasn't naturally rude or mean, and if it hadn't been for the strings attached to it, she'd be grateful. She *was* grateful. She just didn't want to encourage him or make him feel that just because they'd spent one incredible night together they could have any more than that.

And she was still angry with him, still not entirely convinced that his turning up at her hospital was just coincidence, and still very, very vulnerable to his potent charm. Scarily so.

But she let him lead her to his car—not his Italian sports car, she noticed, but a sensible little Alfa Romeo—and she sank down into the soft leather seat and rested her head back, and in seconds she was asleep.

'Wake up, sleepyhead,' Luca said softly, reluctant to disturb her when she was clearly exhausted. 'I need directions.'

'Oh.' She struggled up from the depths of her seat and looked around. 'OK, you're nearly there. Turn left just past that pub.'

'Here?'

'Yes—down here, and turn left there and pull up. This is it.'

He parked outside a pretty little terraced house in a tree-lined street tucked away off the main road, and cut the engine, relieved to see that it was in a very respectable neighbourhood.

'So are you coming in for that coffee?' she asked, but she

sounded grudging and he realised that he still had a very long way to go.

'Am I welcome?'

She sighed. 'You've brought me home. Even I'm not that churlish. Anyway, you said you wanted to talk,' she said, reaching for the doorhandle.

He hesitated. 'When do you work again?'

'Tomorrow, seven-thirty,' she said.

'That's crazy. I can't come in now, it's far too late, we'll talk tomorrow. You need to get to bed.'

Oh, why had he said that word? Something dark and dangerous unravelled inside him, and he wished she'd just get out of the car and go into the house and shut her front door before he carried her through it and onto the nearest flat surface. He gripped the wheel tightly.

'Come on, Isabelle, get out. I'll see you in the morning,' he said, wishing she would open the door, but she hesitated and then turned to him.

'Oh, this is ridiculous, you're here now, and, anyway, I won't sleep for ages after that nap.'

She reached for the handle and got out, and after a fractional hesitation he followed her, going through her front door and into a narrow but well-kept entrance hall, his hands rammed firmly into his pockets. 'I'll make coffee,' she said, heading for the kitchen.

'Can you make that tea?' he said, starting to follow her. 'I've had so much coffee today to keep me awake that I won't sleep. And is there any chance of some toast? I'm starving.'

'Of course. Stay here.'

Stay here. An order, Isabelle setting the limits, taking control of a situation she was unhappy with, he thought, but he stayed, giving himself a little breathing space and taking the opportunity to learn a little about her and her home.

It was small, neat and full of homely touches, but a little tired round the edges. A typical rented house, like so many others, but at least she'd made an effort to make it home. But it was a ludicrous distance from her work, and he was sure she could have found something closer if this new post was going to last any length of time.

But it wasn't his business, of course, and Isabelle would be the first to tell him that, and however frustrating he found it, he was beginning to realise that he couldn't just order her about and take over her life and look after her, because she just wasn't going to let him.

However much he wanted to.

He grunted with frustration. Given the choice—which was never going to happen!—he'd take her home to his house, literally round the corner from the hospital, and install her there with him—in the spare room if she insisted—for the duration of the refurb in her own hospital. And maybe by then he would have enough time to convince her that he wasn't a bad person, and that what had happened when they'd met, that tidal wave of emotion and reaction, had been bigger than both of them.

And maybe, just maybe, they'd find they had a future.

But not yet. It was too soon. She had issues to deal with, and until he could talk her into giving them a chance, they weren't going to move this thing forward at all. So he ignored his frustration and looked around.

There was a photograph on the mantelpiece of a younger Isabelle with a woman who looked as if she could be her mother. They had their arms around each other and they were laughing, and it made him smile. It could have been a photo from his own family, bossy and interfering, but loving and supportive, too.

There had been times when he'd needed that so much. He turned away from the photograph with a sigh, and lowered himself onto the sofa cautiously. He'd sat on plenty of rented sofas in the past, and they were almost without fail too hard, too soft or just plain wrong.

This one was all of them. Shifting to avoid a spring, he leaned back cautiously, rested his head against the cushion and closed his eyes.

It was a good job it was so uncomfortable, or he might just stay here forever…

'Oh!'

She put the tray down and stared at him in frustration. He was asleep, for heaven's sake! So much for a five-minute chat and booting him out of the door. She sat down opposite him in the chair and left him to it while she sipped her tea, telling herself it was out of kindness but secretly grateful for the chance to study him.

He looked tired. His eyes were shadowed, his lashes dark against his olive skin, and he was dead to the world. No wonder pagers were so horribly aggressive and hard to ignore. Nothing else would have got through to him, she was sure, and she wondered how she'd failed to notice just how tired he was.

Probably because she'd either been too busy avoiding him or so busy with a delivery that all her attention had been on her patient. Whatever, she hadn't looked at him properly— had never had the chance to look at him really closely without him looking back, and she felt a little voyeuristic.

It didn't stop her, though. Nothing short of him waking

would have stopped her, and she let her eyes linger on his jaw, with its shadow of stubble that gave him a morning-after look reminding her so strongly of Florence. His nose was strong and straight, but there was a little bump in it where it had been broken at some time. A sporting accident? Or fighting over a girl? She could imagine him doing that, in his teens. And he would have won, of course.

His lips were slightly parted, full and soft and beautifully sculpted, like one of Michelangelo's exquisite pieces; his eyes sat deep in their sockets, his brows a clean, strong arch over them, crafted by a master's hand. She wanted to reach out and touch his face, run her fingers over the warm, silken skin, feel again the rough scrape of his stubble, the flesh and bone beneath. Feel that glossy hair, so dark it was almost black, and with a texture like raw silk.

She could remember the feel of it between her fingers, the soft, thick strands teasing her body as he moved over it, driving her mad with his wicked, clever mouth.

She swallowed and shut her eyes, letting her breath out on a whimpering sigh, and after a moment, when she opened them, he was watching her.

'Are you all right, *cara?*'

'I'm fine. You were asleep—I started without you,' she said, indicating his mug and the pile of buttered toast on the table between them.

His smile was wry. 'We didn't all have the benefit of a catnap on the journey,' he said easily, and sat forward to pick up his tea and a slice of toast.

She curled up, hitching her feet up under her bottom and wriggling back in the chair to give herself a little more personal space. Not that it helped. He was still far too close for comfort, and her thoughts were still recovering from the memory of his mouth trailing over her. She could move away from him physically, she realised, but she couldn't escape so easily from her own head.

'OK—you wanted to talk, so you'd better do it, starting with why you were looking for me,' she said, not allowing either of them to get sidetracked now he was awake, and he leaned back with his tea and regarded her steadily over the top of it.

'I wanted to see you again,' he said simply. 'One night left me with more questions than answers. I felt...' he shrugged, 'unresolved.'

Oh, she knew all about that. She'd tried so hard to resolve it in her mind, to put him out of it, even, but her mind wasn't having any. Unresolved? Oh, yes.

'So you thought you'd come and find me?'

He inclined his head a fraction. 'I had to come to London anyway, to finish off my research. I had a starting point in that I knew the name of your hospital, so I thought I'd try there.'

'So you just—what? Contacted them and asked for me?'

'Yes—and I drew a blank. I didn't know your last name, and so I couldn't give them enough information to be convincing. And I don't know any of the clinic staff there, so I couldn't pull strings. So I asked around a few friends without success, and then I gave up. I told myself you had my number, you could call me again if you wanted to, and you hadn't, so I assumed—but if I'd needed to, believe me, I would have found you,' he said in a voice that left her in no doubt it was true.

'How?' she asked, half-joking. 'By hiring an investigator?'

He shrugged, and she stared at him, seeing in his eyes that it had been a possibility, and shocked by the very idea, but suddenly it seemed to make a lot of sense. 'Is that what you did?'

she asked slowly, a cold chill creeping over her as she realised she knew nothing about him, but he gave a grunt of laughter.

'No. Why would I do that? You wouldn't give me your phone number, you didn't give me your address, and when you rang, you withheld your number. You obviously didn't want me to find you. Even I can take a hint—so, no, I didn't hire an investigator. It was purely coincidence. Richard and I have been friends for years, and he heard I was around and we met for a drink, and I told him I was taking time out and working on my research, so he offered me the job. I'd all but given up any hope of finding you, and I had no idea you worked there until I saw you.'

He sounded sincere, but she still wasn't sure. 'I thought you were working in Florence—in that job they offered you. I never expected you to turn up like that in London and shock the living daylights out of me.'

He frowned at the distrust in her eyes, and the fact that she could think those things of him. 'I'm sorry. I didn't mean to upset you and it really wasn't planned. I just wanted a chance to see you again, to talk to you—maybe spend some time together. Take you out for dinner.'

Take you to bed.

He sighed and scrubbed his hand through his hair, trying not to think about that. 'Look, I promise you, us meeting up again was just coincidence, although there aren't that many maternity units in London so maybe it was inevitable that some point I might run into you, but I've never chased a woman in my life— I've never had to. And I wouldn't contemplate chasing someone who wasn't interested. It's happened to me too damned often.'

She gave a choked splutter of laughter. 'Modesty's not one of your failings, is it?' she retorted, and he just rolled his eyes.

'It's nothing to do with modesty. It's just the truth. I'm a doctor, and I'm not exactly hideous, I'm realistic enough to know that, nor am I on the breadline. It's a pretty potent combination, so I'm told. Frankly I could do without it. And if you really don't want to see me again, I'll accept that and I'll tell Richard I can't take the job. I don't want you to feel you have to hide from me or lie to me or feel threatened, and I'm sorry if I've made you feel like that. I didn't mean to make you uncomfortable.'

She felt a pang of guilt. 'I didn't deliberately conceal anything from you,' she said quietly. 'And we'd agreed we wouldn't see each other again, so I was really shocked when you turned up. I didn't expect you to come looking for me.'

'I didn't expect to want to. I really wasn't going to, but then I couldn't seem to get you out of my head. But you didn't tell me where you were going when your department was being closed down for refurbishment, and you must have known, so you weren't being completely open with me.'

She shook her head. 'I didn't know where I was being moved to and, anyway, it didn't seem relevant. I had other things on my mind.' Things like him. Things like his smile, and the scent of his body close to hers, and the feel of his lips on hers.

She yanked her thoughts back in line. 'But, anyway, that's all beside the point, Luca. I had reasons for not wanting to see you again, that's why I didn't give you my number.'

'What reasons? Is there another man in your life? This guy that hurt you? Or is it all in the past?'

'Is it any of your business?' she asked a little desperately, and he shrugged.

'I don't know. Maybe. If it affects the way you relate to me—

and certainly if there's someone else. I don't poach from another man's territory, and I don't do infidelity, mine or anyone else's. Ever—at least, not knowingly, so if there *is* someone…'

'There isn't. Well, at least, not for me. I told you, I don't—'

'—do relationships. I know. I don't either, not recently. But you—you got under my skin, Isabelle. I've had affairs, but they don't last. They leave me cold—well, not cold, but certainly not hot,' he added, his voice dropping sensually, his accent more pronounced, 'not so hot I thought my clothes would catch fire, so hot I thought I'd die if I didn't have you right then, right there on the walkway above the Duomo in front of the entire city. Not so hot I could hardly get you through the bedroom door before I tore your clothes off so I could feel your skin against mine.'

'Stop! Stop it!' she begged, her hands shaking so much she slopped her tea over her legs. 'It was just craziness.'

'*Si*, I know. But I've never felt like that before. It was the first time in my life I'd lost control, and the first time in my life I felt really, truly alive. And I realised that, after feeling like that, despite whatever might or might not happen with us in the future, I could never settle for less. That's why I wanted to find you—to know if it was real, because it felt real, *cara*. It felt more real than anything ever has before, and I wasn't ready to let it go.'

She didn't know what to say, so she said nothing for a while, just stared into her tea while he ate toast and sipped his tea and his words went round and round in her head.

'Isabella?'

She looked up at him, shocked by his honesty and the strength of his reaction. And her own. 'Luca, I don't know what you want me to say.'

'I don't want you to say anything particularly. I want you to keep an open mind. I have no idea if this could last, but I want to find out. I want to get to know you, give you a chance to get to know me. Give us a chance.'

'You want to have an affair?'

He gave a soft grunt. 'Perhaps? Maybe not, not yet. But I feel as if I've lost my mind, having a crazy, white-hot fling with a beautiful Englishwoman who's bewitched me and turned my brain to mush. That why I tried to find you, and why I decided to come stay in London for a while longer.'

She frowned and ignored the crazy white-hot nonsense because she didn't dare think about it, and focussed instead on the one fact she hadn't registered. 'Longer? What do you mean, stay longer?'

'I've worked here off and on for years. I was doing some research here from October, then I went home for Christmas and someone told me about the job in Florence. I'd nearly finished my research, I was ready for the next step in my career, and I went for an interview. They offered me the job, I walked out of the hospital—and then I met you.'

'So—what happened with the job? Didn't they mind delaying your start?' she asked, irrationally disappointed at the thought that he'd be going back to Italy soon, but he shook his head.

'It's irrelevant. I turned it down. I wanted to find you.'

'But—why, Luca?' she asked, stunned. 'Why throw away your job in Florence for someone you didn't even know? It was only one night. How could you have let it change your whole life?'

He laughed softly. 'Because it did. Because I can't get you out of my head, *cara*. You've bewitched me. I had to find you, but I couldn't bring myself to have you hunted down by an investigator—or maybe it was that I was too proud to admit that you'd walked away from me, so I left it to the gods. I thought maybe if I hung around long enough, I might run into you. Which I did.'

By accident, if she could believe that. She still wasn't sure she could. Whatever, he was now working alongside her—potentially for months, she realised—with nothing to stop them from exploring this relationship. Except her fear and lack of trust—and she still wasn't really sure she could believe his story about how he'd found her. It all sounded too innocent to be plausible.

'So—having found me, what do you think happens next?' she asked, her heart pounding with a mixture of anticipation and dread, and he shrugged, his eyes curiously veiled.

'We see where it goes.'

Her heart stalled. 'Where what goes?'

His voice was soft and low, teasing her senses and sending a shiver through her. 'Whatever it is, this feeling between us that won't seem to go away.'

Her heart started again, and she swallowed hard, refusing to allow herself to be tempted by the serpent, no matter how sweet and juicy the apple.

'Why, Luca?' she asked with a touch of desperation. 'Why me?'

'I don't know,' he said softly. 'Why me? I have no idea why it happened, but it did—and we both felt it that night. I wasn't alone, Isabella. You felt it, too, and I won't let you deny it.'

She couldn't, but she didn't want to think about that night. She sucked in a breath. 'I acted out of character. I don't do that—don't have relationships and certainly not one-night stands.'

'Perhaps because there's never before been that much temptation,' he suggested quietly, and she swallowed hard.

'God, you've got some ego there, Luca.'

'It's not ego. It's the truth. We couldn't help ourselves, *cara*. Either of us. It was meant to be.'

Was it? She didn't want to think so, but at the time, every look, every touch had been enough to make her forget her own name.

'That still doesn't mean we've got a future,' she said, and his mouth twisted into a wry, humourless smile.

'Maybe not. But it wasn't only me. I knew it was crazy, but I couldn't let you go without knowing how it would be between us.'

'You didn't have to come and find me, though. I told you I didn't want a relationship. It was just one night.'

'No. It was more than that, Isabella, and you know it.'

Oh, God. *Isabella*.

'No. We agreed. That was all it was meant to be. I didn't want to see you again,' she lied, 'didn't want a relationship, and I still don't.

'I told you at the time, I don't do relationships.'

'So how come you're on the Pill?'

She coloured softly. 'To regulate my cycle,' she told him frankly, holding his eyes even though she clearly wanted to look away. 'Nothing more.'

'Why not? You're a beautiful woman, Isabella. You should be living your life, not just going through the motions.'

'I *am* living. I don't need a man in my life to do that. We don't all have to indulge in indiscriminate sex to validate us as human beings!'

'There was nothing indiscriminate about that night. It was incredible—every moment of it. It was wonderful.' His voice sounded rough to his ears, and he swallowed. 'You were wonderful—and you deserve to be with a man who can appreciate you.'

'Not if I don't want it.'

He sighed softly. 'But you did—and it moved you to tears. When was the last time you cried when you made love, Isabelle? When was the last time it made you weep?'

Her eyes filled, and she looked away. 'I was tired. It was just—'

'That it reached something inside your heart that hasn't been reached for years? If ever?'

A tear slid down her cheek, and he reached across the table to her, cupping her chin in his hand and tilting her head back so he could see her tortured eyes. 'Who was he, this man who hurt you, *cara?* What did he do to you that you're so afraid to love again?'

He felt her flinch slightly, and she swallowed. She looked cornered, but she wasn't telling him why. Not yet. Not now. But he would find out, in the end. She'd tell him when she was ready.

His touch was so gentle, his thumb grazing slowly back and forth over her chin, his eyes concerned, and it made her want to cry. She didn't do that. Couldn't allow it.

She stood up and went to the door and opened it. 'I think it's time you went home,' she said unevenly, and waited while he put down his mug, got to his feet and brushed past her, turning on the step to stare down into her eyes.

'I'm sorry,' he said quietly. 'I didn't mean to upset you. Whoever he was, he's hurt you badly, but don't judge us the same. Give me a chance, Isabelle. Let me prove myself to you.'

'Luca, I can't. I wish you hadn't found me.'

'I know. I'm sorry it upset you, but I'm not sorry I found you again, and I'll never be sorry that I met you, that we shared that time together, and I know you feel it too.'

'No.'

'Don't lie to me, *cara*,' he murmured gently. 'And especially don't lie to yourself. You deserve better than that.'

And because he couldn't help it, because she was just inches from him, her chest rising and falling and her eyes wide with a nameless emotion that made his chest ache to comfort her, he leaned in and kissed her.

For a moment she softened, but then she dragged her mouth away and pressed her hands against his chest, right over the ache.

'Luca, please, just *go!*' she pleaded, and with a sad smile, he stepped back and moved away from her.

'*Buonanotte, Isabelle.* Sleep well. I'll see you tomorrow.'

And turning on his heel, he strode down her path, closed the gate gently behind him and got into his car.

Her lips still tingling from his kiss, she shut the door, leant back against it and listened to the sound of him driving away into the cold, wet night, and then she closed her eyes, wrapped her arms around her waist and cried, because she still wanted him just as much as she ever had but she was too afraid to dare to love him, and no amount of reasoning was going to change that.

CHAPTER FOUR

SHE WAS DREADING seeing Luca the next day, but she needn't have worried because by the time she arrived he was already in Theatre with an emergency C-section, and so after handover she went to meet the patient she was taking over.

Jodie Kembroke was a woman who had been due to deliver at the other hospital and, like Isabelle, had been transferred. She'd met her two years before when she'd delivered her first baby, and the only reason she was in the consultant unit here now was because this baby was breech.

'It only turned last week and they say I have to have a section. I'm so cross,' she confessed. 'I really wanted to try and deliver naturally, but they won't let me. Hospital policy or something. It's dangerous. And now I've gone into labour early, so Rob's trying to find a babysitter, and I want him here.'

And with a sinking heart she realised that she was going to have to involve Luca in this one, regardless of her urge to avoid him.

'Well, it's certainly safer for the baby to deliver it with a section,' Isabelle told her honestly, 'because coming this way the head doesn't get a chance to mould to your pelvis, but you've only just had a few twinges and you're not dilating fast, so we'll watch you for a while and get Mr Valtieri to come and see you as soon as he's out of Theatre. He shouldn't be many minutes. You can discuss it with him. It's his call really.'

And with any luck, she thought, trying to ignore the little flutter in the region of her heart, he'd let her deliver the baby vaginally. She'd never seen a breech delivery, and everyone these days was so risk-averse they didn't dare to let the mothers try.

But Luca didn't strike her as someone frightened of anything, and most particularly not authority. And hadn't one of those papers she'd seen from him on the internet been about breech births?

She wished now she'd paid it more attention, but she'd been so busy missing him she hadn't really read it. There was a glimmer of a memory, though, and she had a feeling he was pro rather than con. Well, they'd soon find out, she told herself, and felt another little flutter around her heart.

So stupid. So, so stupid, after their conversation last night. He'd come too close, seen too much, and there was no way she was going to let him any closer, but on the professional side, if he'd let Jodie deliver naturally, she'd be ecstatic.

Assuming the hospital authorities would allow it, of course.

She left a message for him at the central workstation to contact her as soon as he was out of Theatre and then collected a jug of ice chips for Jodie because she was on nil by mouth pending her C-section, but by the time she went back into the room things had moved on. A lot.

'I can feel his bottom,' Jodie said, and the fact that she said 'his' made Isabelle fairly sure she knew what she was talking about. A quick glance confirmed it. And that meant it would almost certainly be too late for a C-section by the time they'd moved her to Theatre, so she was going to have her baby there on the ward, with only Isabelle to look after her, because everyone else was running flat out.

And Isabelle had never done this before.

She hit the button, opened the door and was about to call for help when Luca turned the corner.

'What's up?' he asked, following her back in and assessing the situation instantly. She filled him in fast as he turned off the call button, reached for the hand gel, then the gloves, his quiet calm filling her with confidence. 'OK, I'm Luca, Jodie, I'm going to have a quick look at you—what's the history, Isabelle?'

'Second baby, scheduled for elective C-section—I delivered the first two years ago with no problems, but things have just speeded up in the last few minutes,' Isabelle told him, wondering now about the old saying of not wishing for something lest you get it.

Well, it looked like she was getting her breech delivery, right now, and she just hoped Luca wasn't cross that she hadn't called for him sooner, but he was showing no signs of it, just smoothly, quietly taking over.

'OK, I don't want to move you to Theatre, Jodie,' he said calmly. 'I don't think it's necessary and you're doing this beautifully, so we'll just carry on here. Now, I want the baby's back facing the ceiling, so I'd like to get you onto all fours, if you can, so his back is upwards and his bottom will hang down and curl his spine nicely as he comes out, which means his head is in the best possible position for delivery. And we'll just let nature take care of it for us—OK?'

'OK,' Jodie panted, and with their help she turned over onto her hands and knees. 'Oh, my God, it's coming!' she screamed, and Luca placed a firm, gentle hand on her back and rubbed it slowly, his palm moving in rhythmic, soothing circles over her sacrum, relaxing her pelvis. Just as Isabelle would have done.

'It's all right, just let go and breathe with it. Let the baby's weight do the work. You're doing really well. Good girl. We don't touch anything,' he added softly to Isabelle, 'we just watch and catch. He's a good colour, so I'm not worried at all at the moment.'

And just like that, under his own weight and with Jodie pushing valiantly on command, little baby Kembroke was born, yelling his head off, just as his father was ushered into the room.

'Oh, Jodie,' he said softly, and tears coursed down his cheeks. 'You did it! Oh, you clever girl!'

'Let me hold him,' she said, rolling onto her back and reaching for her baby, safe in Luca's big, gentle hands.

'He's beautiful. You did really well.'

'And I didn't need a stupid section,' she murmured, lifting her son to her breast, and Isabelle met Luca's eyes and surprised a wistful, yearning look that she'd never expected to see there.

'Gets me every time,' he said under his breath to her, his grin a little off kilter, and she gave a ragged little laugh.

'Me, too,' she confessed. 'That's why I do it.'

'Me too.' He smiled at the couple and stripped off his gloves. 'I can leave you to finish, can I?' he said, watching her inject the Syntocinon, and she nodded, but in truth she would have liked him there a little longer.

'Can we talk through it later? Over coffee?'

'Sure, come and find me when you're done here,' he said, and left her to it.

* * *

'I've never seen a breech delivery before—it was amazing,' Isabelle told him, her eyes shining, and he was stunned.

'I think that's shocking. You should know how to, at least. It isn't necessary all the time to do a section—it's just being over-cautious, and then when you have to go with it because of an emergency or a precipitate labour or because the lift gets stuck, nobody knows what to do.'

'I knew the theory, but—'

'—it's not the same as the hands-on,' he said with a smile, getting into his stride because breech delivery was a bit of a hobby-horse for him. 'We're too quick to intervene, and sometimes we need to go back to basics. Look at the treatment for club foot. From the 1950s we've been using casting and stretching in combination to correct the deformity slowly, with good results, then they discovered surgery and the outcome isn't nearly as good in the long run. And now— eureka!—we're going back to casting and it's all got much more sensible again.'

'But breeches are different. If you get it wrong with club foot, nobody dies.'

'Nobody dies with breech if you're on the ball and don't take stupid risks. Everybody wants to fiddle with it, and sometimes if it's a bit slow you need to hook the legs and arms down gently, but usually it happens by itself, and it's just wonderful to watch.'

'Do you ever need forceps?'

He shrugged. 'Some people use them. I hate them, but there are times when there's no choice. Late babies are more of a problem because of the size of the head, but Jodie's baby was a little early, not too big and it went fine. And her recovery will be much faster.'

'So do you ever do a C-section for breech?'

'Oh, yes, of course I do. There are some breech presentations you just can't deliver, and I'd rather do that than end up using forceps, but I don't have a blanket ban on vaginal breech deliveries, because I think it's ridiculous.'

'It's hospital policy here.'

He grinned. 'I'll pretend I didn't hear that,' he murmured, and she felt her heart flip over.

He bent his head forwards, fiddling with his coffee, chasing a bubble round on the surface. Then he looked up and his eyes met hers. 'Have dinner with me tonight after work.'

She shook her head, so tempted it was ludicrous but too vulnerable to dare to allow it. 'No, Luca. Please. Don't start this again.'

'Lunch in the canteen?'

She gave a rueful laugh. 'I won't get a lunch break. It's a miracle I've got a coffee-break.'

'You work too hard.'

'No. I work three days a week—and it suits me. And now I have to go back. Thanks for talking it through. It was really interesting. I'm glad you didn't rush her to Theatre.'

'Why? No point. And it's a pleasure. Think about lunch.'

'I can't.'

'Rubbish. I'll come and find you.'

She was right, of course. There was no time for a lunch break, so she was glad Luca had fed her a pastry with her coffee. She stole time for a cup of tea and a bar of chocolate in the ward kitchen at five, but apart from that she'd had nothing all day.

That didn't mean she hadn't seen Luca. Far from it. He'd been haunting the ward, and now Sarah had a patient who had been in established labour for ages and was getting nowhere fast, and she was assisting her.

'I'm going to have to call Luca,' she said eventually, and Isabelle nodded.

'I agree. Want me to page him?'

'Could you?'

'Sure.'

She went out to the workstation and dialled his number, and he walked out of Richard's office and cocked an eyebrow at her. 'Are you calling me?'

'Yes—Sarah's got a problem that needs you. She's in three. I'll be back in a second, I've got to get something. I won't be long.'

He nodded and went into the delivery room and found the other midwife there with a woman and her husband. 'Right—we have a problem?' he murmured, and Sarah nodded.

'Yes—she's just exhausted. I'm sorry to call you but we've tried everything and the baby's beginning to struggle.'

He nodded. 'OK. Let's see if we can't give her a hand.'

Isabelle walked in just in time to see the slickest Ventouse delivery she'd ever seen, and in seven years she'd seen a few. And Sarah, of course, was all over him. Well, she was welcome, she told herself, and tried not to feel jealous when he smiled at her friend.

It was nothing personal. He smiled like that at everyone, but it had the same effect on them all. Us all, she thought, wishing she was unmoved by it, but she wasn't, not even slightly.

Then he lifted his head and smiled at her, and her heart skidded into hyperdrive. He was checking the baby, chatting to the mother and father, and he excused himself, stripped off his gloves and came over to her.

'I love the Ventouse. It's my party trick,' he said with a grin. 'Like pulling a rabbit from a hat.'

'The Great Valtieri? Maybe you should get your own magic show—not that you're blowing your own trumpet or anything…'

'Of course not,' he said, managing to look mischievous and affronted all at once, and so sexy that her tongue dried instantly and stuck to the roof of her mouth. She swallowed hard to free it and wiped her hands down the sides of her scrubs.

'Right, I need to get on,' she said to break the silence, and then Sarah came over to them.

'Um—we usually leave the proud parents alone and have a cup of tea at this point,' she said. 'Want to join us?'

'Thank you,' he murmured, and his grin turned to a smile that brought colour to Sarah's cheeks and made Isabelle's heart flutter. 'I could murder a cup of tea—and any chance of some toast?'

'I'm sure there will be, we can't have our resident magician fading away,' Isabelle said briskly. 'I'll just finish off in here and make sure everything's OK. You two go ahead, I'll join you in a minute,' she said, and, turning on her heel, she went to check on the mother and baby, and all the time that smile of Luca's was still echoing through the far reaches of Isabelle's body and making her heart pitter-patter.

So stupid. So many if onlys. She wished for the millionth time that she could dare to trust him, but his charm came so easily to him she wasn't sure she could. And there was still the problem of her own reluctance to commit…

'That man is incredible!'

Tell me about it, she thought, and rolled her eyes. 'If you say so. Where is he?'

'Oh, he had something to do, he'll be here in a minute. But

he is just—that was so slick. You know, that baby's head was just tipped back the tiniest bit, and she was so tired she just couldn't get it to shift—and as you know, we'd tried *everything*, Izzie. Then he just strolled in, grinned at her, attached the cup and pop! Out it came. He hardly even lifted it. He made it look so damned easy!'

She picked up a slice of toast that Sarah had just buttered and bit into it. 'It's all in the wrist action,' she mumbled round the toast. 'I expect it's from twirling all that spaghetti,'

Sarah chuckled. 'And he's so gentle with them. I've never seen a doctor treat a woman more carefully, with so much— I don't know, respect, I suppose. Almost reverence.'

And then she looked at Isabelle, and her eyes widened in distress. 'Oh, God, I can't believe I'm being so tactless. I'd completely forgotten—'

'Sarah, it's fine,' Isabelle lied, trying not to think about those reverent hands and how they'd touched her with tenderness and respect as well as passion. 'I met him, we spent the day together—it was nothing.' Except it hadn't just been the day, it had been the night, too, and that was so much harder to forget. 'Really,' she repeated, forcing her voice to sound casual, 'it was nothing—nothing out of the ordinary at all.'

And then she looked up and saw Luca standing there in the doorway. His face was like stone, and without a word he turned on his heel and walked away, and for some inexplicable reason she wanted to cry.

Nothing out of the ordinary.

Dio! He wanted to put his fist through the wall, slam doors, hurl something good and heavy through the nearest sheet of glass.

Instead he went into the office, shut the door with exaggerated care and threw himself down in the chair.

Nothing out of the ordinary.

He closed his eyes and made himself breathe slowly and deeply. She didn't mean it, of course. She was just being defensive, because of whatever it was in her past that she wouldn't give him access to. And she was angry with him for finding her. But she wasn't indifferent. He knew that, knew it in his bones, and slowly the anger dissipated.

She was just saying those things to Sarah. She didn't mean it, didn't believe it. It *had* been out of the ordinary—so out of the ordinary that it had made him throw away all his plans for the future and fly back to London on a wild goose chase to find her.

Nothing out of the ordinary?

No. Isabelle was trying to ignore her reaction to him, but she was very, very far from indifferent—and that gave him hope. Oh, it wouldn't be easy, he was under no illusions about that. But he'd get there. Especially if he could ever get her to tell him her story.

And now he had that out of the way, he was suddenly starving. Maybe there was some toast left in the kitchen…

'Right, time to go home.'

She sighed and glared at him. 'Are we going to have this fiasco every single night?' she asked crossly, but he just gave her that lazy smile and shrugged.

'I don't know. Are we? I hope not. You've had a long, busy day and you're late, which I suspect is not unusual. And I know you haven't eaten anything remotely like a vegetable all day, so I've made you supper, and then afterwards I'll run you home.'

'You've—I said no!' she protested, but he wasn't listening, just tucked his hand into her elbow and steered her to the lift.

'No arguments. You're no use to anyone hungry and exhausted, and besides, I've gone to a lot of effort.'

'Well, I could have saved you all of that. All you had to do was listen to me a little harder.'

He grinned. 'I have problems with my hearing sometimes.'

'Evidently. You need to learn to lip-read. I—said—no!' she mouthed, but he just laughed and shut his eyes, and she found herself smiling.

Not that it mattered, because his eyes were shut—or so she thought. But then she caught the gleam of an eye through his lashes, and realised he was laughing at her.

'Crazy woman,' he murmured, his hand tightening on her arm in an affectionate squeeze. 'Come on, it'll be overcooked.'

'What is it?'

'Pasta with chicken and roasted Mediterranean vegetables in tomato sauce.'

'Bottled?'

He looked shocked. 'Shh! Not so loud. My mother would be appalled. And you need to know I'm frightened of my mother.'

That made her laugh. The very idea of Luca being frightened of anyone, not least his mother, was ludicrous. And she was absolutely starving.

'Where's your car?' she asked, looking round as they emerged through the door.

'At my house. It's just round the corner. It's quicker to walk.'

'Oh! You live really close,' she said as he stopped just two streets away and opened a garden gate in front of a tall modern townhouse.

'Yes—it's handy. I hate commuting, so I bought it.'

She stared at him blankly. 'For a few weeks?'

He gave a short laugh and explained. 'No. I bought it four years ago, when I worked here, and I've used it as a base ever since. Come on in.'

And, opening the door, he ushered her inside.

Isabelle looked around, taking in the soft earth tones and the sense of light and space, conscious of a sense of order and quietness that pervaded the house. 'It's very tranquil.'

'It is. I love it. It's my favourite place. Well, except my family home in Tuscany. That'll always be top of the list, but this is mine, and that makes it special. Can I get you a drink? Coffee? Tea? Wine?'

'Have you got any juice?'

'Sure. Apple and mango?'

'Lovely.'

She followed him through to the kitchen and sniffed appreciatively. 'Oh, it smells really good.'

'Of course. Did you really think I'd be allowed out into the world without knowing how to fend for myself? Even if it is out of a bottle,' he added in a stage whisper.

She tried not to smile, but not well enough because he winked at her, took a bowl of salad from the fridge and pulled a dish from the oven, bubbling with cheese and tomato sauce and smelling utterly fabulous.

Her stomach rumbled, and he pointed to the breakfast bar, a thick, sleek glass shelf on shiny chrome supports with tall chrome and leather stools tucked in underneath. 'I thought we could be uncouth and eat in here,' he said, and she looked around at the kitchen, with its sleek granite worktops and high-gloss cupboards, thought of her house and how utterly uncouth it was in comparison to this undoubtedly extremely expensive kitchen, and her heart sank.

She'd not given a moment's thought to his financial status, but one serious look at this kitchen brought it all home to her with a vengeance.

He was so completely out of her league, so overwhelmingly different, and there was no way he would ever be interested in her except as a passing fancy. The only reason he was interested in her at all was because she was playing hard to get. Treat 'em mean, keep 'em keen—wasn't that the saying? Except she wasn't trying to be mean, and she didn't want him to be keen, she wanted him to leave her alone, because he was going to break her heart all over again and this time, she knew, it would be so very much worse.

'What's wrong?'

'Nothing. I'm just really hungry,' she said, and turned her attention to the food. It wasn't that hard. She was ravenous, she discovered after the first mouthful, and his cooking, bottled sauce or not, was sheer genius. So she ate, and he talked about breech presentations and cases he'd seen and the research he was doing, and gradually she forgot about his money and remembered only that he was a brilliant doctor, kind and gentle and yet persuasive when he needed to be, and brave enough to take a risk if he felt it was justified.

There were all too few like him, she mused. Far too few. But that didn't mean she was going to let him lure her into a relationship, and she realised she was getting dangerously close to that. Sitting in his kitchen eating food he'd cooked for her while she finished her shift was all too cosy, and she had to be mad to do it.

She pushed her plate away, nothing left on it but a touch of the rich tomato sauce, and smiled at him. 'That was really lovely. Thank you. And now I hate to be rude but I ought to be getting home.'

'No dessert?'

'Did you make one?'

He chuckled. 'No. But I have gelato—proper Italian ice cream, made by my cousin's family, that will make your toes curl.'

'What flavour?' she asked, hating herself for weakening, and as if he knew that, he leant closer and murmured in her ear.

'Ripe, juicy strawberry with fresh cream, or deep, dark chocolate—irresistible…'

Oh, lord. It was only ice cream!

'Chocolate,' she said, but then hesitated.

'You can have both,' he said, luring her with a double whammy, and she weakened.

'A little of each—not too much. And then I really must go.'

It was, as he'd promised, enough to make her toes curl. And she had a sudden picture of him feeding it to her in bed, a sensual image that made her want to whimper. She pushed the bowl away before she actually licked it, and braced her hands on the edge of the glass shelf.

'Luca, I have to go now.'

'Of course. Leave this lot, I'll sort it later. Come on.'

And he ushered her out of the door to his car and drove her home through the hubbub of London at night, until at last they turned into her quiet little street and he pulled up outside her house and cut the engine.

'I think you owe me coffee,' he said, a teasing smile playing round his mouth, and she thought, Damn him, he's going to be charming and he's hard enough to resist under normal circumstances!

'I gave you coffee last night.'

'So you did. It must be a tradition, then, and you can't mess with tradition.'

He was irrepressible, but she wasn't falling for it.

'I need my sleep. I didn't get enough last night.'

She saw the brow twitch, and tried to glare at him but he wasn't impressed. Instead he just grinned, and she ignored him and opened the car door.

He was there almost before she'd got out of the car, shutting the door behind her and escorting her down her little path. 'Just seeing you safely home,' he murmured as she turned to protest, and she caught the scent of his cologne overlying the raw, male essence that was so much more intoxicating.

'I'm safe. You can go now. Thank you for my supper.'

'You're welcome. When will I see you again?'

Her heart hiccuped, and she reminded herself that he wasn't asking her for a date and she wasn't going even if he was asking. 'I'm back in on Friday,' she told him, but his nearness was getting to her and she swallowed, and his eyes flicked to her mouth.

'I want to kiss you,' he murmured, and she shook her head. 'No.'

'You didn't say no in Florence.'

'Perhaps I should have done, then we wouldn't be in this crazy position now.'

'You think? I don't agree. We were destined to happen, *cara*.'

She shook her head. 'No. It was just sex, Luca,' she said, her heart pounding because of his nearness, because of the scent of his body drifting over her in the cold night air. 'That was all.'

Nothing out of the ordinary.

Her earlier words came back to taunt him, echoing in his head as they had been all day, and his mouth twisted in a fleeting smile. 'I don't think so,' he murmured. 'I don't think there was anything *just* about it. I think it was exceptional.'

'No.'

'Yes,' he said softly, and because he couldn't resist it, because she looked delectable and there was a trace of chocolate ice cream in the corner of her mouth, he leant in towards her and let his lips brush over hers.

His hands were rammed in his trouser pockets, hers hung by her sides. There was nothing holding them together but the touch of their lips, and as he stroked his tongue against her mouth, her lips parted for him and he was lost.

He freed his hands, tunnelled them through her hair and cradled her head to steady her, and with a tiny whimper she fisted her hands in his shirt and hung on while his mouth plundered hers, the silky glide of her tongue against his driving him wild.

For a second—for one crazy, heat-filled second—he contemplated pushing her inside, kicking the door shut and carrying her upstairs to her bedroom. He could do it. She wouldn't protest. But she would hate him tomorrow, and that wasn't part of his plan, so instead he just kissed her until his control was stretched so thin he couldn't trust himself another moment, and then he lifted his head and stared down into her feverish eyes, his chest heaving.

For a moment she said nothing, but then she stepped back, her hand coming up to cover her glistening, parted mouth, and he could see it was trembling.

'Why did you do that?' she whispered.

'What? That goodnight kiss?' He smiled a little tightly, his anger coming back now, fuelled by frustration. 'It was just a kiss—nothing out of the ordinary. Isn't that what you said to Sarah?'

She swallowed hard, her eyes filling as his words registered. 'Oh, Luca—I'm so sorry. I didn't mean it—not like that. And I wasn't talking about us—about that night. I hadn't told Sarah anything, just that I'd met you. I wasn't gossiping, I promise. I was trying to stop her getting the wrong idea about us.'

He laughed softly. 'Don't you mean the right idea? The idea that we couldn't leave each other alone in Florence and it's no better here? Because it isn't, *bella,* you know that. Even though you want me to go, you couldn't stop yourself from kissing me back.'

'That's not true.'

'Don't lie,' he murmured. 'You were with me all the way.'

'That isn't the point!'

'I would have said it was very much the point,' he argued softly, but she closed her eyes and made a tiny sound of frustration that just inflamed him further.

'Please—just go,' she said, wondering if she would be destined to say this to him every night until either she gave in or he left the country.

Except she wasn't giving in, even if her legs were like jelly and her heart was thundering against her ribs and her body was aching for him.

And then at last, when she was ready to scream, he took a step back, and then another, and finally he turned without a word, got back into his car and drove away, leaving her standing on the doorstep wondering how on earth she was going to survive working with him for the next however many weeks.

Luca spent the next few days contemplating his tactics.

If she really meant it, and she wouldn't see him, he'd have to find some other way to win her round, because he fully intended to do so.

He could easily tell himself that whatever they'd had between them on that mad, crazy night had been a little touch of magic and nothing more, and he could set it aside if necessary and work with her without compromising his professional integrity.

But he didn't want to, and it wasn't an option. So what if she said she didn't want him? He knew she did—he just had to convince her to try it. He'd had a taste of the wild, all-encompassing passion that could exist between a man and a woman, and he would settle for nothing less now. And that meant winning Isabelle.

She'd done him a favour, kick-starting his life again, saving him from a lonely and tedious life when there was so much more out there, and he wasn't going to walk away from it now, when he'd only just found her again. He'd spent six weeks convincing himself he was over her, and it had been a lie. He wasn't, and he didn't want to be.

He wanted Isabelle, and he'd have her. Somehow.

Then she walked onto the ward on Friday morning, her auburn hair swinging round her shoulders, her cheeks rosy from the cold, those beautiful amethyst eyes challenging his, and he felt a kick in his gut that told him more clearly than anything else how important this was to him.

He wasn't ready to give up on her—not even slightly. He

hadn't moved on, he couldn't forget the night they'd spent together. He wanted her as much as ever—not the wild and generous lover, curiously, although his need for her was never far away, but her, this beautiful, principled and wounded woman—and he was going to convince her to give them another chance.

'Isabelle,' he said as casually and professionally as he could manage, 'I have a patient I'd like your help with.'

'And good morning to you, too,' she retorted.

He gave a wry laugh and started again. 'Good morning. How were your days off?'

'Lovely, thank you. Peaceful. You were saying?'

'I have a patient. It's her third pregnancy, she was admitted about an hour ago with intermittent contractions, and she needs a little TLC. Her first delivery was textbook normal, then she had a C-section for a placenta previa, and she's going to try for another normal delivery, but she's scared. I've squared it with your ward manager, and I'd like you to manage her delivery.'

She met his eyes challengingly. 'Why me?'

'Because you're good.'

'Sarah's good,' she said bluntly.

'Sarah's off today.'

'Well, Helen, then. Any of them. They're all good.'

'I want you. You're the best.'

'That's rubbish.' She turned away, heading into the staff-room. 'I'll see you in a minute,' she muttered, and shut the door in his face.

He shrugged. Well, she was reluctant, but she hadn't told him to take a hike. And he could wait for her to come round.

Just so long as she didn't take too long, because he was an

impatient man, he was discovering, and the clingy little sweater she'd been wearing under her coat was enough to push him over the brink.

He went into the ward kitchen and made himself a cup of coffee. He'd been in the hospital since six, waiting for Isabelle and trying to convince himself that she would be fine if he didn't go and fetch her, and so far today he hadn't had time for a drink. And if he didn't get some caffeine down himself soon he was going to be ripping heads off.

'Right—where's this woman?' Isabelle said, appearing in the doorway in scrubs, and he offered her his mug.

'She'll keep for a moment. I'll fill you in. Want this?'

She shook her head. 'No, I'll pass. It's a bit early for coffee and I haven't really got time to make tea. I'll have a glass of water. So, tell me, how frequent are her contractions?'

'Every three minutes. It could be quite quick.'

Great. Isabelle swallowed and put the glass down, trying to psych herself up. She could do with a slow start today. She'd been feeling a bit iffy when she'd woken—edgy about seeing him again, of course—and she'd had to struggle with the bus and the Tube. She'd even been frustrated that he hadn't turned up to give her a lift, of all the contrary things…

'OK, I'll go and get handover on her and introduce myself. I take it you're happy to leave me to it?'

'Of course.'

'Right. I'll keep you posted.'

'Thank you.'

Good grief, so formal, so civilised, and yet under it all, the memory of that kiss was seething and simmering like a wild thing. She walked away, deeply conscious of his eyes on her back, trying to halt the sway of her hips as she walked. The last thing she wanted was for him to feel encouraged. She was still furious with him for kissing her, but not nearly as furious as she was with herself for responding.

Oh, damn it!

She went and found her patient.

'I hate you! Don't you dare come near me! This is all your fault!'

'Well, excuse me, but it wasn't me who forgot to take the pills regularly.'

'Hey, guys, come on, now. Lindsey, calm down, nice slow breaths. That's it. Good girl.' She shot a smile over her shoulder at the husband, standing at the foot of the bed ramming his hands through his hair and looking helpless. 'It's OK. It's not personal,' she said softly as Lindsey breathed her way through a nasty contraction. 'You'll have your baby very soon.'

'Is she all right?'

'Yes, she's just in transition. Everything looks lovely.'

His shoulders dropped, and he closed his eyes and gave a soft laugh. 'You know, once we got over the shock we were really pleased about the baby. It was just a bit unexpected, hearing her talking to me like that.'

'Ignore it. She'll be all smiles in a few minutes.'

'I won't. I hate him,' Lindsey muttered between breaths.

'Of course you do,' Isabelle said soothingly, rubbing her back and eliciting a deep groan of relief. 'Mike, why don't you do this for her?' she suggested, and then Lindsey's eyes flew wide open and she stared at Isabelle wildly.

'I have to push!'

'OK, that's fine, you're ready now. Nice and steady, you can remember how to do it.'

Behind her she heard the door open quietly, and she knew without looking round that it was Luca, and she was relieved, because one of the team was off sick and she was on her own again today and if anything went wrong...

'OK?' he murmured softly so as not to distract Lindsey, and she nodded.

'She's just gone into second stage.'

'May I stay?'

'Please do.'

'You can defend me,' Mike said, smiling at him and maybe a bit relieved to have his support. 'Apparently this is my fault.'

Luca chuckled softly. 'Isn't it always? The man can never win.'

'Well, it is his fault, so don't you join in and gang up on me—oh, hell, I want to kneel,' Lindsey said, dragging herself up the bed and hanging on to the headboard, her body draped over the pillows. And moments later, with very little fuss, their daughter was born, and Isabelle felt the familiar wave of emotion sweep over her.

'Congratulations,' she said warmly, settling the tearful, smiling Lindsey back against her pillows and putting the baby to her breast. 'She's absolutely beautiful, aren't you, sweetheart?'

Luca patted Mike on the back. 'Well done, guys. I thought you'd be fine. I'll leave you in Isabelle's capable hands. I'll get you a nursery nurse to help.'

'No hurry,' she said, because she enjoyed this moment, and once she was happy that everything was as it should be, she'd leave them alone for a while to get to know their baby.

'Aren't you glad now that I've got a lousy memory and kept

taking my pill late?' Lindsey was saying with a huge smile on her face, and Isabelle laughed.

'See? I told you you'd be forgiven,' she said to Mike.

'Oh, of course he's forgiven,' Lindsey said with a smile, 'but it's a good job we lead a fairly sober life, because I had no idea I was pregnant for months. I was still taking the Pill but I was feeling iffy, and I just thought I must have a virus and then I got over it and started to eat like a horse and put on weight. And then I looked at myself one day in the mirror and the penny dropped. All those late pills, and look where it got me, little one,' she said, her voice softening as she turned her attention to the baby again. 'In here with you! And you're just gorgeous.'

In the middle of checking the placenta, Isabelle froze. Late pills? A virus? Feeling iffy? And her last period had been really light…

Oh, dear God, no!

She felt a wave of panic and disbelief, and having checked that the placenta was intact and that Lindsey and the baby were both looking well, she left them to it for a moment, heading for the staffroom.

'I've just put the kettle on—fancy a coffee now?' Luca said as she approached the kitchen.

'Not really,' she said, unable to look at him. 'I'll get something in a minute, there's something I have to do.'

And diverting to the supplies, she took a box off the shelf, slipped it into her pocket and walked off the ward.

'Luca?'

'Isabelle? What's the matter?'

'Nothing, but—I need to see you.'

He sat up, turning off the television, his heart starting to pound slowly, his mind in freefall trying to imagine why she was calling. 'When did you have in mind?'

'Are you free now? I've just finished work. I could come to you.'

'Sure, I'm here. Can you remember the way or do you want me to come and get you?'

'No, stay there, I'll come,' she said, and headed for the exit.

Luca tidied the sitting room and put his empty mug into the dishwasher while he waited. He couldn't imagine what she wanted. He could dream, he could fantasise, but he had no real idea, and her distant greeting this morning—her distance all day, really—hadn't given him much fuel for the fantasy.

The bell rang and he let her in, taking in her pallor and the tight line of her lips. It didn't look like she was about to give in to him, he thought with regret, and hung her coat on the end of the banisters. Maybe she just wanted to talk—perhaps to tell him whatever it was that was getting in the way of them having a relationship. Hallelujah! And then maybe they could make some progress.

'What can I get you to drink?'

'Um—have you got any fruit juice?' she asked, part of her wanting to stall and the other part wanting to get it over with quick before she lost her courage.

'Sure. Apple and mango again?'

'Lovely,' she said, following him and hugging her elbows.

He poured her a glass, made himself a coffee then led her into the sitting room, gesturing to the pair of leather sofas that sat at right angles to each other. She perched on the edge of one, and he sat on the other, and silence settled over them.

'So why did you want to see me?' he said eventually, and

she swallowed hard. There was no easy way to do this, so she might just as well get it over with. Taking a deep breath, she looked up and met his eyes.

'I think I might be pregnant.'

CHAPTER FIVE

LUCA FELT THE blood drain from his face. 'Pregnant?'

'I—I think so.'

His heart thudded hard against his ribs, her words so un-expected they'd caught him completely off guard. 'And it's mine?' he asked, his voice rough even to his ears.

She stared at him, her eyes blank. 'Well—of course it's yours.'

'There hasn't been anybody else?'

'No. No! Not for years. You know I don't do relationships, and I certainly don't do one-night stands.'

'But you're on the Pill,' he challenged, pushing her, while the blood roared in his ears and the sense of déjà vu threat-ened to swamp him.

'To control my cycle. Nothing else. Luca, if I am pregnant, it's definitely yours.' And he could tell from her eyes that it was the truth.

He felt the shockwave go through him, and closed his eyes briefly, setting his coffee down with a little clatter into the saucer before looking up at her.

But her eyes were on the cup, and she swallowed hard. 'Bathroom,' she muttered, and, crashing her glass down onto the table, she fled into the hall.

'On the right,' he yelled, following her, but she'd found it, slamming the door behind her and leaving him in limbo. Did he follow her? Hold her hair? Or give her her dignity? He waited, while the emotions roiled through him, his heart pounding, until he heard the loo flush and water running.

Then he tapped on the door and met her wary eyes as she opened it, his heart beating heavily in his chest as they stood looking at each other in silence. Action and reaction, he thought, and asked the question that had been burning a hole in him for the past few minutes.

'Isabelle, when you say you *think*...'

'I did a test.'

Hell. 'And?'

'It was a bit inconclusive.'

Well, the last few minutes wasn't, he thought drily, and felt a skitter of nerves. 'When was your last period?' he asked, his voice deadly soft as he tried to stay calm.

She gave a tiny, defensive shrug. 'Last week. But it was light,' she added. 'So was the one before.'

'So—it's nearly seven weeks since Florence, which would make you...'

She swallowed. 'Nearly nine weeks pregnant—if I am.'

Oh, she was. He could see it a mile away, but he had to know. He took a slow, deep breath. 'Do you have another test with you?'

She nodded numbly. 'In my bag. Luca, I'm on the Pill,' she said, her voice a little desperate.

'And did you take it punctually?'

She nodded her head slowly. 'Pretty much, but it's only to regulate my periods, so I'm not religious about it. And that morning, I took it just before we boarded the flight and then

I was airsick in the turbulence and I felt so dreadful I just didn't think about it until now—'

She broke off, and he stabbed his hand through his hair. 'And I—' He'd been so inflamed with passion that he'd forgotten his own name. Damn. He picked up her bag from the floor and held it out to her. 'Just do the test, *cara,* please. We need to know this. *I* need to know it.'

She took it, her fingers shaking, and rummaged for a box— a pregnancy test kit from the ward. He recognised it instantly. She handed the bag back and shut the door, and he waited. And waited. What seemed like hours later, when he was about to tear the door down and go in and find her, she opened it and walked out, her face ashen.

'Well?' he asked, his voice tight.

She handed him the little white stick.

'Congratulations, Luca,' she said unsteadily. 'You're going to be a father.' And then she burst into tears.

He didn't even look down. One glance at her face had been enough to tell him the answer, but he'd needed to hear her say it. And his reaction was not at all what he'd expected. In the midst of the shock, somewhere buried down there amongst a whole plethora of emotions and complications and sheer, blind terror, a tiny flicker of joy burst into life.

He was going to be a father. He felt his eyes fill, and blinked hard, scarcely daring to hope, but he *knew* Isabelle was pregnant. He was an obstetrician. He knew the signs, knew it wasn't possible to fake the chalk-white skin with the faint sheen of sweat, the nausea and its inevitable result—and sure, she could have produced a positive pregnancy test stick but he'd seen her go into the loo with an unopened packet and break the seal.

He *knew*.

And now he had to think of the future.

'We need to talk.'

Talk? She nearly laughed out loud, but it would have been more than a little hysterical, so she just clamped her mouth shut and headed out of the hall, walking into the sitting room and standing there staring unseeing through the window, arms wrapped tight around her waist, while the emotions crashed through her like a tidal wave.

'Go on, then, talk.'

He laughed, an odd, fractured sound that scraped on her nerves. '*Cara*, we *have* to talk. This is going to happen, and we have to face it. What alternative is there?'

Shooting myself? Ringing my mother and telling her I've been as stupid as she was? Scrolling back through all the drugs and chemicals and foodstuffs I've been exposed to in the past few weeks?

'Going home to bed,' she said, suddenly feeling incredibly tired and tearful and wishing Luca would go away so she could curl up in the corner and howl.

She got her wish. His pager went off, and muttering something Italian and no doubt rude, he put a gentle hand on her shoulder. 'Later. I have to go back to the hospital, but you can stay here,' he said. 'Go and rest now, I'll come home as soon as I can. Use my bed.'

'I can't. I have to go home.'

'No, you can't do that awful journey in this state—or work the hours you've been working. It's ridiculous when you're sick.'

'No, Luca,' she said, turning to face him and meeting his eyes with defiance. 'I'm not sick. I'm pregnant. There's a difference, and I have no intention of being treated like an invalid—and before you even think about it, don't you *dare* go and tell my colleagues to get them to take my workload off me, or I swear to God, I'll kill you with my bare hands.'

He felt a reluctant smile tugging at his mouth. 'I'm terrified.'

'You should be.'

Their eyes locked, and then he gave a little shrug and sighed. 'OK, I won't say anything, for now—but only on condition you're sensible. And that means lying down now and waiting for me to get back, at the very least. Is that clear?'

He could see the struggle in her eyes, but finally she nodded. 'All right, I'll wait. But here. I don't need to go to bed.'

He hesitated, but then his mouth firmed and with a curt nod he turned on his heel and walked back into the hall. She turned back to the window and watched him walking down the street until he disappeared into the night. It was raining now, fat drops hitting the window and streaming down it like rivers of tears, and resting her head against the cool glass, she closed her eyes again and pressed her lips together.

Pregnant. Just like her mother, pregnant, single and alone.

Self-pity washed over her, and she firmed her spine and told herself not to be melodramatic and ridiculous. Her mother had been much younger and she'd had no training, but Isabelle had a good career, in a field where working part time was perfectly possible, her maternity leave would be assured and there was a crèche available to solve her childcare needs.

OK, it wasn't the future she'd hoped for, but it would be a good future, and at least she had the house. She'd told her mother it wasn't necessary to put it in her name, but now she was grateful, because in the end it would be the thing that above all else gave her security.

She—*they*—would be all right. And that was all that mattered.

Pushing herself away from the window, she lay down on the sofa under a lovely snuggly throw and tried to sleep, but her mind was whirling. She sat up again and noticed a newspaper on the coffee table, opened at the puzzle page. He'd started the crossword, filled in a few numbers on the Sudoku, but she could finish them off. It would keep her mind occupied till he got back…

She was asleep, her eyes shadowed, the long, thick lashes dark crescents against her pale cheeks. Her mouth was closed but her jaw was relaxed, and her lips looked soft and full and kissable.

Resisting the urge, he put the bowls down and sat beside her, his hip brushing against her abdomen as the cushion sank under his weight and she rolled towards him. His child was in there, he thought, feeling the warmth of her body against his hip, cradled in the bowl of her pelvis, a tiny baby, slowly growing in the shelter of her body, and it was suddenly real to him. Please, God, let everything be all right. He couldn't bear it if it wasn't.

He rested his hand on her hip and stared at her, the woman who was carrying his child, and a fierce wave of protective tenderness washed over him, catching him by surprise, because this was for her, not for the child. His feelings for the child were a given. His feelings for the mother were much less ordered and would take time to sort out. But for now, he had to feed her.

'*Isabella?*' he murmured. 'Wake up. I've cooked for you.'

'No,' she moaned, and buried her face in a little cushion.

He took it away from her. 'Yes. Come on, you need to eat. Sit up—here, it's just boiled rice and vegetables. Nothing too flavoured, but you must eat. You've had nothing all day.'

She struggled upright. 'I'm not hungry,' she grumbled, but she shoved the hair out of her eyes and took the bowl and ate, reluctantly at first and then more eagerly as it became obvious it wasn't going to be instantly rejected by her body.

'Better?' he asked, searching her face for clues, and she smiled a little wanly and nodded.

'Yes. Thank you. I was getting a bit shaky.'

'You mustn't let yourself get hungry. That's the worst thing. Low blood sugar's a killer. And don't have coffee, or cola, or strong tea or even dark chocolate. Caffeine can increase the risk of miscarriage significantly—and it's probably why it and many other potentially harmful or potentially bacteria-laden foods can trigger nausea in early pregnancy—'

He cut himself off, realising he was lecturing her, telling himself not to get over-protective, but she just gave a funny little smile.

'Luca, I do know this. I'm well aware that we're programmed to avoid the dangerous things when the foetus is most vulnerable.' She rolled her eyes. 'Don't worry, it's very effective. I won't be drinking coffee ever again, I don't think. Just the smell is enough to kill me.'

'Was it my coffee today?' he asked, suddenly realising that when she'd run away, he'd been drinking it, and she nodded. He let out a harsh sigh and shook his head.

'*Bella,* I'm sorry. You should have said.'

'I didn't know until it happened.'

'Well, it won't happen again,' he said with a twisted smile. 'Come on, you need to go to bed now, you look exhausted. And I will review your rota, whatever you say. These long days are no good for you, and I don't want you working nights.'

'The nights are fine, Luca. I like working nights. They're quiet and peaceful.'

'But you need a regular routine, so you can eat properly and your body can settle into pregnancy without constant disturbance.'

'Luca, it's my body! I'll decide.'

She had that mulish look about her chin again, and he let it go. For now. There was plenty of time to fight with her. Years and years and years, if he had his way.

'Come on, let me put you to bed, and then I've got to go shopping for things that are good for you, and in the morning we'll talk.'

'I'm not staying here,' she said, looking panicked.

'Don't be silly. It's really late, and I'm on call. I can't take you home and the Tube's about to shut. Please, *cara*. Don't try and go. I'm only trying to help you.'

She hesitated, reluctant to give up too much independence but too tired in the end to argue, so she nodded. 'OK, if you insist—but I'm not sleeping with you. I'll sleep here.'

'Don't be silly. I've got two spare rooms, the beds are made. Why don't you have a bath while I'm shopping?'

A bath. That sounded so tempting. She nodded. 'OK.'

'Not too hot, though. It'll make you sick.'

She shut her eyes. 'Luca,' she said warningly, and he got up off the sofa so that the warmth of his body was removed from her thigh. And, stupidly, she missed it.

'I'll run the bath for you,' he said, ignoring her warning, and disappeared upstairs. A few minutes later he came back down. 'It's ready for you now,' he said, and then he held out a hand and eased her to her feet.

'I've put you out a T-shirt in the bedroom at the top of the stairs, and the bathroom's just opposite. I won't be long,' he promised, and headed for the door, tossing his keys in the air and leaving her alone with her thoughts.

Or not quite alone.

Her hand slid down until it lay over the baby, curled protectively around her tiny, defenceless child, conceived in an unpremeditated and ill-considered moment of wild passion and now destined for the sort of childhood she herself had had.

Oh, well, it hadn't done her any harm, and she'd always known she was loved, but she felt a flicker of fear for the future of her child. What if something should happen to her? What would happen to her baby then?

Exhausted with emotion, longing for the oblivion of sleep and promising herself that she'd phone her mother in the morning and talk to her, she went upstairs, undressed in the bedroom he'd got ready for her and went into the bathroom.

And stopped dead.

He'd run her a bath, she'd known that, but he'd also lit candles on the side, and put a few drops of lavender oil in it from the bottle on the window sill. She bent and tested the water with her fingers, and sighed. Tepid. Well, not quite, but certainly not a long, hot soak. But it would do—and he was quite right, a hot bath would only make her feel sick. And it smelled lovely.

She eased herself into it, lay back and sighed with relief.

Five minutes, she promised herself. Even Luca couldn't shop that quickly…

The house was in silence.

He went into the kitchen, put away all the shopping and then crept upstairs to check on her. Her bedroom was empty, her clothes dropped where she'd taken them off, and so he walked across the landing to the bathroom and eased open the door.

She was asleep, lying with her knees rested to one side and her hands curled over her abdomen, and just the sight of her brought a lump to his throat.

Not the surge of lust he'd expected, but another wave of tenderness. He wanted to wake her, to lift her from the water and dry her and put her to bed, but he knew she'd only get mad at him, so he pulled the door to and tapped on it gently.

'Isabelle? Are you in there?'

There was a little gasp and a splash, and he could picture her sitting up and clutching her arms across her breasts.

'Um—yes. I'm not decent—hang on.'

'It's OK. I'm going back downstairs. I was just letting you know I'm back.'

'Oh. Thanks, Luca. Goodnight.'

Goodnight?

Stifling a strange disappointment, he went downstairs, made himself a drink and sat in front of the television, trying to focus on the news and failing. He picked up the paper that was lying on the table and finished the Sudoku he'd started. Except there were some numbers that weren't in his writing, and he realised she'd been doing it. Which was why it was wrong, he thought, and corrected it with a smile. Then he finished the crossword, filling in the last two words just as she appeared in the doorway.

'Hi,' she said, tugging at the hem of the T-shirt and triggering the surge of lust he'd expected earlier. He wanted to tug at the hem of it, too, but he'd tug it the other way.

He dragged his eyes up to her face. 'Kettle's hot. I bought some herbal teabags—I thought you might like them. There's a selection on the side. Choose one and I'll make it for you and bring it up.'

'I'll do it. I was going to take the paper up—I wanted to finish the crossword.'

'Ah.'

Her eyes flew up to his and she snatched it out of his hand. 'Have you done it? You have, haven't you? You rat— *and* the sudoku!'

'It is my paper—and I'd started it,' he pointed out fairly, but she wasn't pacified.

'That's not the point—I'd spent *ages* working out the last clue!' she retorted, then threw the paper down again with an exasperated sigh and spun on her heel, giving him a flash of thigh and the peep of a warm, pink buttock scantily covered by lavender lace as the hem flicked up and then dropped back into place, and he felt a surge of desire that nearly took his legs out from under him.

'I think I'll go to bed,' she said from the doorway, her chin up in the way he was beginning to find rather endearing.

'You could sit here and talk for a minute,' he suggested, but as he'd expected she shook her head.

'No way,' she said briskly. 'I'm going to get my tea and then I'm going to bed. And don't go getting any ideas. I might be having your baby, but that doesn't mean we're together. Nothing's changed.'

He gave a soft snort. Funny, that. He hadn't doubted it for a moment. Unfortunately…

She woke to the sound of movement in the kitchen, and a wave of nausea that took her by surprise. She got cautiously out of bed, but just the act of standing had her running to the bathroom, and when she lifted her head it was to see Luca's legs in view, his hand extended with a handful of tissue for her to blow her nose and wipe her eyes.

Her teeth were chattering with reaction, and he sighed and bent to help her up.

'I'm sorry, *cara*,' he murmured, guiding her back to bed. 'I meant to come to you in time.'

'In time?'

'*Si*—with breakfast.'

'Oh, God, don't,' she said, feeling her throat close at the very suggestion, but he just tucked her into bed like a child and handed her a glass of fizzy water.

'Sip it slowly.'

She tasted it, tried a little, then put it down. 'OK. What's that?' she asked, eying the plate on the bedside table suspiciously.

'Apple. Chilled apple slices. And watermelon. Just nibble them. They'll give you some sugar and settle you, and the clean flavour is good, according to my sister.'

She sat up abruptly—not wise. 'You've told your sister?'

He gave her a crooked smile and shook his head. 'No. But because I'm an obstetrician, I discussed it with her when she was pregnant. I have a mental note of things that help and things that definitely don't.' His smile twisted. 'All caffeine products are banned from my life now,' he said wryly, 'so forgive me if my temper gets a bit ragged. It's not personal.'

She wasn't looking forward to his ragged temper, but it knocked spots off the smell of coffee. She took a proffered apple slice and nibbled it cautiously, and after a moment the rebellious churning in her stomach subsided a little and she tried another bit, then more, the watermelon this time.

'OK?'

She nodded. 'Yes—thanks.'

'I'll fetch you some dry toast and herbal tea, and then we'll talk.'

He left her with the plate of apple and watermelon slices and went away, and she lay there and wondered what he wanted to say. A long, almost sleepless night hadn't helped refine her thoughts, except to reinforce her initial fiercely protective reaction. Would he share it? Or would he try to talk her into—no! Her mind recoiled from the thought, but she realised he hadn't mentioned the baby again, and she had no idea how he'd feel about her keeping it. How would he see his future involvement in her child's life—or wouldn't he?

She had no idea, but there was only one way to find out, and the sooner the better. She threw back the bedclothes and went to wash.

Luca shut the kitchen door, opened the back door and made some toast, then once the smell had gone, he made a cup of ginger and lemon tea, because ginger root was supposed to suppress nausea, and put a scrape of sugarless fruit compote on the toast and took it upstairs, tapping on the bedroom door as he pushed it open.

He should have waited. Clearly he should have waited, because she was naked, in the act of threading her second foot into the pair of ridiculously lacy French knickers he'd glimpsed last night that had sent his blood pressure through the roof, and as she shrieked and straightened up to cover herself, he was treated to the gentle sway and bounce of her breasts, the nipples a glorious dark rose, darker than they had been before and bigger, pebbling in the cold and making his lips ache to suckle them.

She glared at him. 'You're supposed to wait when you knock,' she told him crossly, and he swallowed and tried not to choke on his tongue.

'You were supposed to stay in the bed until I brought you breakfast,' he reminded her, his self-control falling apart under the strain of standing there with her all but naked just feet away from him.

'Well, you can go now,' she snapped, whirling round and reaching for the bra she'd placed on the bed.

Lace, to match the knickers, in the same pale lavender as her eyes, and he thought, *Dio,* I'll never be able to look at her eyes again without thinking of the underwear. Swallowing hard, he turned on his heel and headed back downstairs to wait for her, her breakfast tray still clutched in his hands, forgotten.

And he'd imagined all those weeks that he was over her? Not in his wildest dreams.

She came down a few moments later, looking fragile and wary but with her head held high, and he'd never wanted a woman more in all his life.

She perched on a stool at the breakfast bar and he pushed the tray towards her. 'Eat. And drink the tea. It's lemon and ginger. It'll soothe your stomach.'

She sipped it, pulled a face and nibbled the toast. 'Did you sleep?' he asked, and she nodded.

'Yes—a bit. Not much. I was thinking.'

'Me, too. I was thinking that I want you out of that awful rented house with the hideously uncomfortable furniture, and into my house where at least I'll be able to look after you. It's only sensible—it's right next to the hospital, and you can't do that journey while you're pregnant, it's much too long and dangerous.'

She was staring at him, her eyes flashing fire, and she set the cup down with a wobbling hand and met his eyes. *'That awful rented house,'* she said in a measured tone that made him realise he'd overstepped the mark, 'happens to belong to me. And I will not move out of it. I know the journey's difficult, but I can get a cab—at least for the end of the day.'

It was *her house?* He could have kicked himself. 'I'm sorry. I didn't realise the house was yours. I just assumed—'

'Well, don't,' she said crisply. 'I don't need your assumptions, or your instructions on how to live my life. In fact, I need nothing from you at all, except one thing,' she went on, her chin lifting. 'In case you're worried about it, I've decided to keep the baby,' she told him, throwing up a subject that hadn't even crossed his mind, 'and I don't want anything from you, so don't even think about getting all macho and insisting we get married, because the answer's no. I just want your name on the birth certificate.'

CHAPTER SIX

LUCA FELT HIS jaw drop.

Of all the things she could have said, that was absolutely the last he was expecting.

Sucking in a lungful of air, he shut his mouth and tipped his head on one side.

'Is that all?' he said softly, wondering how something that should have been amazing and incredible and a source of celebration could have been reduced to something as technical as a name on a piece of paper. 'You want my name on the baby's birth certificate?'

'Yes. For the baby's sake. My father died when I was two, and because my mother wasn't married to him, she had no protection in law, no legal status as a widow, no right to his estate. She'd been buying our house—that *awful* house—for some while, though, so we weren't homeless, but his wife's family were dreadful to her.'

He was still wincing over awful, but that got his attention. 'Wife?'

'He was married—to someone so emotionally unstable he couldn't tell Mum about her. And then he died and his wife found out, and it was horrendous for my mother. I didn't know anything about it, of course, I was only a few years old, but I gather it was dreadful. And I don't want that happening to my child.'

No wonder she was so wary. It was enough to make any woman suspicious of men. But he wasn't her father, and there was no wife waiting to take revenge.

'Well, if it's any consolation there's no wife and I have no intention of dying.'

She glared at him. 'Will you please be serious?'

'I'm being totally serious. I've never been more serious about anything. But you have to know, Isabella, that I intend to be very much more to my child than a name on a birth certificate, whether I'm married to you or not.'

'Well, I won't marry you, so don't even think of asking me.'

'I won't—not yet. I think getting married just because you've made a baby between you is a very shaky way to start a marriage, but I would ask you not to rule it out for the future.'

The glare changed, softening into confusion. 'Luca, I can't—' She bit her lip, her eyes filled with pain. 'I don't want to get married. I don't want that sort of relationship.'

'Well, you should have thought about that before you had unprotected sex, shouldn't you, *cara?*'

'I didn't.'

'Yes, you did. You told me you were on the Pill, but you weren't, not reliably—not religiously taking it on time, because you weren't taking it for that reason, and if I'd known that I would have made sure you took the morning-after pill.'

'I was taking it—I was airsick.' she said drily. 'Not even you could have altered the turbulence.'

He gave a brittle laugh. 'Possibly not, but now I'm facing the reality of becoming a father to a baby whose mother won't contemplate forming a stable, loving relationship with me.'

'Luca, you can't love me!'

'Why? Why can't I?' he demanded.

'Because you don't know me,' she said, her voice distressed, 'and I don't know you. I *can't* love you.'

There was something in her voice that troubled him, and he reached out a hand to cover hers.

'Why can't you love me, *cara?*' he asked softly. 'If you give yourself time, then maybe…'

'It isn't time,' she admitted, her eyes fraught with emotion. 'And it's not that I can't love you, Luca—it's that I can't trust you. I can't trust any man.'

'Because of your father?'

'Partly.'

'And?' he coaxed. 'The other part?'

She shook her head, and he sighed softly and lifted her hand into his, cradling it between his palms, willing her to talk to him, to let him in. 'Who was he, Isabelle? What did he do to you? Tell me, *tesoro*. Talk to me.'

She swallowed hard and tilted her chin in that endearing way, and he saw her eyes were clouded with tears. For a long time he thought she wouldn't tell him, but then she turned and met his eyes defiantly.

'He was my fiancé. He changed his mind, just before the wedding, and went back to his old girlfriend. They got married, and the last I heard they had two children and they'd split up. Now you tell me, why should I trust a man after my father and my fiancé have both proved that they can't stay faithful?'

And that was why, of course, she was wary—not only because of her father, but because of her fiancé, and Luca wanted to find the man and kill him for hurting her so badly.

'Oh, Isabella,' he said softly, and without waiting for an invitation, he swung round on the bar stool and drew her into his arms. For a moment she sank against him, then she straightened up and turned away.

'Luca, stop it! I don't want to lean on you. I don't want to need you.'

'Why? What's so wrong with needing me? You can't do everything alone.'

'Why? My mother did.'

'And did it make her happy?'

She sucked in a fraught little breath and turned her head away. 'Luca, I can do this.'

'Of course you can. But you don't have to, and I don't want to be shut out, Isabella. This is my baby, too. I need to be part of its life, on a daily basis—starting now. And you're going to have to learn to trust me.'

'How? How on earth am I supposed to do that? Luca, I *can't!* I don't know you.'

'So get to know me. Spend time with me, *cara.* Come to Italy with me and meet my family, see my home, have a bit of fun. We'll start today—we'll go out for a walk, get some fresh air, feed the ducks—anything you like.'

She hesitated. It seemed like a lovely idea—and if nothing else, she had to get to know the man who was the father of her child. He couldn't remain a stranger to her. So she nodded, and said, 'Yes. All right. But—just that. Just spending time together, no—'

She broke off, and he smiled wryly. 'No reruns of Florence?' She nodded. 'OK. That's fine. It's better. Sex is too distracting. We'll stick to other fun stuff.'

So they did. They went out, via her house so she could change into jeans and trainers and a thick fleece, and they went for a walk on the park near her house and fed the ducks and he made her eat lunch—nothing elaborate, just a simple sandwich in the sunshine outside the pub.

While he was in the pub paying the bill his phone rang, and she stared at it dubiously. 'Gio,' she read, and bit her lip. His brother—or one of them.

'Hello?'

'Well, that's not Luca.'

'No. He's in the pub, he won't be a moment. Can I get him to call you?'

'In a minute. Who's that?'

'Isabelle.'

'So he found you.'

She blinked. He knew about her? 'Um—yes. We're working together.'

His brother laughed softly. 'I knew it. So how much do you know about my brother, Isabelle?'

'Not much,' she confessed. 'Not enough, really.'

'Well, don't hurt him. He's been through enough, and he hasn't had a relationship that I know of for years. Many, many years. Well, not one that's lasted more than a few weeks. But he's a good man, and you seem to have got right under his skin. I've never seen him like he was that morning, when he'd left you at the airport. And when he realised he'd missed your call—well, he was pretty mad with himself. He wanted to talk to you.'

'It wouldn't have made any difference, I didn't want to see him.'

'So—what's different? What's changed?'

Oh, lord. She couldn't tell him. 'Um—we're working together,' she said, flannelling desperately.

'Not today, if you're at the pub. So I assume you're seeing each other.'

'Sort of,' she admitted, wondering how much of this she should be sharing with his brother and when Luca was coming back.

'Well, don't worry. He's a good guy, and he's free—and personally I'd be only too delighted if you got together. He needs a good woman to save him from himself.'

'But you haven't met me.'

'I don't need to. I've only got to hear his voice when he talks about you. I think you might be what he's been waiting for all his life.'

Luca appeared at her side and arched a brow questioningly, and she turned away, filled with confusion.

'You can't—he can't know that.'

'I don't agree. I think he can. And I really hope you'll give him a chance, because of all the people I know, he's the best, most decent, honest, reliable man—and the kindest.' He hesitated, then went on, 'You have to know he's been hurt in the past. I don't want to see that happen again. But just a word of advice—if you hurt him deliberately, or cheat on him or trick him in any way, you'll have me to deal with—and I don't lose in a court of law. Get him to call me, can you?'

'Um—he's here. Luca, it's your brother.'

She handed the phone over and stared at him, trying to read his face. When had he been hurt? And how? Who had hurt him? Some woman. *I don't want to see that happen again.* Her eyes filled with tears and she turned and blinked them hastily away.

'Luca?'

'Yes, Gio. I hope you didn't scare her to death.'

'I don't know. If she scares that easily, she's no good for you. But if you're getting into this as deep as I think you are, you'd better let me get you a pre-nup organised—and I'm serious about this. We need to talk about it. After what happened—'

'Sure. If it's relevant—which it's not at the moment, I'll call you. *Ciao.*'

He hung up and met her eyes again. 'Well? What did he say?'

'Nothing much. I'm sorry I answered your phone, but I didn't know if it was important.'

'That's fine, but I know Gio, he never says nothing. So what did he say?'

'He seems to think the sun rises and sets on you,' she said, and he laughed a little roughly and sat down beside her, slipping the phone back into his pocket.

'I'm sure he didn't say any such thing.'

No, he'd said that he thought Luca had been looking for her all his life. Was it possible? Could it be true? And could she trust him?

'He was very protective.'

He laughed at that, too, but there was something guarded in his eyes. 'Protective? Just what *did* he say?'

'Only that you'd been hurt.'

His mouth tightened. 'He talks too much. Anyway, it's irrelevant and it was years ago.'

'How many?'

'Ten? It doesn't matter. He had no business discussing it with you.'

'He didn't,' she corrected. 'He just…'

'What?'

'Warned me off, I think,' she said thoughtfully. 'But only if I meant you harm. He must love you very much. I can't imagine what it's like to have a brother.'

'Suffocating,' he said frankly, 'and I have two brothers and three sisters, so you can multiply that by five,' but then he smiled and touched her cheek gently with his hand. 'Ignore him. He's just a lawyer. He spends his life immersed in the criminal mind. It distorts his vision.'

She smiled, as she was meant to, and then shook her head. 'Luca, I can't just marry you because of the baby.'

'Of course not. I realise that. And I'm not offering marriage yet. I wouldn't do that until I was sure of my feelings, and yours. But give us a chance—please. We're having a good day today. Let's do it again, see if we have what it takes to make a stable home life for our baby. See if we can fall in love.'

She gave him a sad little smile that twisted something inside him. 'Oh, falling in love with you isn't the problem, Luca,' she said softly. 'I fell in love with you that first night. It's trusting I have difficulty with. Trusting any man. And that won't come easily just because I want it to.'

He felt a surge of hope, then, that they might come out of this with something good, something honest and decent and lasting—because she did want it to, if only he could persuade her to take that leap of faith. And she loved him.

'Come to Italy with me, meet my family. Ask them all about me. They'll tell you the truth—especially my brothers. They won't hold back. You'll get chapter and verse on every time I borrowed their bikes or stole their girlfriends, and my father will tell you how I used to take his car and return it with an empty fuel tank so he'd run out on the way to the petrol station. You want the truth about me, warts and all, ask my family.'

'That's very brave,' she said, wondering if she'd be so honest or daring, and he just gave a crooked grin and shrugged.

'There's a lot at stake, *cara*. It's going to take some courage, from both of us, but the rewards—' He broke off and swallowed, and she could see the emotion in his eyes. 'I want to be a good father, Isabelle. Please don't deny me the chance.'

It was that which swayed her. The sincerity in his eyes, the genuine wholehearted endorsement from his brother. The not-even-thinly veiled threat.

'All right,' she said softly. 'But I'm scared, Luca. I don't trust easily, and it's so long since I've had a relationship I'm not sure I know how.'

'Then we'll find out together.' He smiled tenderly and held out his arms, and she moved into them, resting her head on his shoulder and feeling instantly at home. How could she? How was it possible to feel so much at ease with him when her life was in such chaos?

Or maybe it wasn't in chaos at all. Maybe, for the first time in her whole life, it was actually on the right track...

She spent the rest of Saturday with him, but she wanted to go home in the evening.

'Stay with me. Let me look after you,' he said, but she refused, and so he drove her home, picking up some food for her on the way.

He put it in the fridge, closed the door and shook his head. 'There—that should last you a day or two, you stubborn girl. I wish you'd stay with me.'

'I'm fine, Luca. Really. I'll make sure I've got a flask of iced water by the bed, and some crackers and an apple. I'll be fine.'

'Well, let me stay here, then.'

'No. Really, I'll be fine.'

'I'll come and see you before you get up.'

'You don't need to.'

'*Si,* I do. I want to. It's the least I can do. This is my fault.'

'How can it be your fault?' she asked, remembering her patient Lindsey telling her husband Mike that it was his fault and him reminding her that she'd been the one to forget her pills.

'I should have taken care of you,' he said gruffly, 'not been so wrapped up in my own needs that I forgot something so basic and simple as protecting you when we made love.'

His words curled round her heart, and she felt a fissure open up in her defences. 'Luca, I was there, too. It wasn't just your fault.'

His hand came up and cradled her cheek, and his eyes were sombre. 'Nevertheless, I should have been the one to take control of that part of it, and I'm sorry to have put you in this situation, but I *will* stand by you, Isabella. I will be here, and if and when we marry, it will be for ever. I will never leave you, or divorce you, or let you down intentionally, and I will absolutely, categorically, never be unfaithful. It isn't the man I am.'

His words nearly reduced her to tears, but he had such faith in their ability to make this work, and she wasn't sure she could share it. Not yet.

'Can we just take one step at a time?' she asked with a fragile little laugh, and he smiled and cupped her cheeks in his hands.

'Good idea,' he murmured, and, bending his head, he feathered a kiss over her mouth, teasing her lips apart with a soft stroke of his tongue so that she opened to him with a tiny sob of need. How could she want him so badly? Need him so damned much, after so short a time?

She didn't know. She just knew that his kiss, his touch, his arms were what she'd been waiting for her entire life, and nothing had ever felt so right.

'*Isabella,*' he groaned, his fingertips shaking as they traced her jaw, his eyes on fire. 'I have to go.'

'No,' she said, her hands holding him against her, and after a breathless moment, he gave an untidy sigh and wrapped her hard against his chest.

'I *have* to go. You aren't ready for this. We already know we're good in bed. You need to get to know me, *bella,* know if you can share your life with me, and this is just a beautiful distraction. Come on, let me go. We agreed.'

He squeezed her gently, then let her go, and she could have cried.

'I'll come back tomorrow,' he promised. 'We'll go shopping for you.'

'Shopping?' she said, dazed. 'What kind of shopping?'

He shrugged. 'Clothes for our holiday? We could go to Harvey Nichols or Harrods.'

She felt her jaw sag. 'I've never been there in my life!' she said. 'And besides, why do I need clothes? I have clothes.'

'Enough clothes? No woman has enough clothes.'

She ignored the teasing smile. 'I have plenty. Why would I need more?'

'To take to Italy?' he said softly. 'To meet my family? We— well, no, we don't exactly dress for dinner, but we change into something a little smarter. And if we're there a week or so…'

Oh, lord, he was serious! She'd thought he was joking, but clearly not. 'I don't know how much holiday I've got,' she flannelled. 'When are you thinking of going?'

He shrugged. 'Soon? A week? Two? We'll have to take a look at the rota.'

Her eyes widened. 'Two weeks? What about booking?'

'Booking what? We'll stay in Tuscany with the family.'

'But—we have to get there.'

He just smiled. 'I'm sure we'll find a flight,' he murmured. 'I'll see you tomorrow. Sleep well.'

And with a gentle, lingering kiss, he left her, feeling just a teeny bit like Alice falling down the rabbit hole…

'So—what do you need?'

Isabelle shrugged and laughed a little wildly. 'I have no idea. You tell me. I'm quite happy to go with what I've got.'

'What have you got?'

She shrugged again, running a mental eye over her wardrobe. Not that she needed to, it was sparse enough to see with one quick glance. 'I've got a nice dress that I feel good in. And a couple of pairs of trousers that are quite smart, and some pretty tops. How cold is it in your parents' house?'

'Not cold, but it can get draughty. You'll need jumpers, perhaps a couple of little jackets? And more than one dress. We may be invited out, and we'll go for lunch, maybe go out for dinner. You'll need quite a few changes for all that.'

She thought of her lovely little dress, and sighed. 'Luca, I really don't see the point. I am what I am.'

'Of course you are, and I don't want anybody to think anything else, but I don't want you feeling under pressure because you haven't got anything to wear. And if you have only one dress…'

'I won't feel under pressure. But I don't want to go today. I'll get something next week on my days off.'

'No. This was my idea.'

'Then I'm not going to Italy.'

She'd folded her arms, and she had that mulish look on her face again, the chin tilted up, the eyes flashing a challenge that did nothing except give him an overwhelming desire to take her straight to bed.

'OK. We'll do something else today,' he suggested, saving the shopping trip for another day when she was feeling less combative. Maybe in Florence, if she agreed.

She hesitated, then nodded. 'All right. Can we go out into the country and take a walk by the Thames? I love walking in the countryside and to be honest fresh air is much more appealing than trailing round stuffy shops. And yesterday was such fun.'

He gave in, knowing when he was beaten. For now. 'Come on, then, let's go, and we'll have lunch somewhere in a pub by the water. Happy now?'

She smiled, her eyes softening. 'Happy,' she said, and his heart melted. Tucking her coat round her shoulders, he ushered her out to his car, buckled her in and set off.

They had a wonderful day. The sun shone on them, the water sparkled and they found a lovely pub right on the river for lunch.

And Luca was like he'd been in Florence, flirting with her, attentive, funny and just plain gorgeous, and she found herself falling headlong even further in love, despite her best efforts.

Would marriage to him be so bad? She didn't know, but it was irrelevant, she told herself, because he hadn't asked her, anyway.

Until they got back to her house, and he made her a drink and sat down beside her on the sofa and took her hand in his. 'So, *cara,* have you enjoyed the weekend?'

'You know I have. It's been lovely.'

'And could you see yourself spending other days like that with me? All of them?'

Her heart speeded up, and she searched his eyes. 'What are you saying, Luca?' she asked softly, confused and stupidly, ridiculously hopeful.

His mouth twisted into a wry smile. 'I believe I'm asking you to marry me,' he said gruffly. 'Only I'm not doing it very well, if you can't work it out. So—do you think you could? Marry me, and spend your life with me, bringing up our child? There would be all sorts of advantages—a huge family, for both of you, for a start. I know that's something you lack, and something I could provide with bells on. There would be lots of little cousins for the baby, and devoted uncles and aunts and grandparents—have you told your mother yet, by the way?'

She shook her head, still wondering if he was proposing that she marry him or his family, and wondering if there was actually a difference or if it might be one and the same thing.

'You should. She needs to know. And so do my parents, but I'd like something a little more concrete to tell them— preferably that we're going to be married. But that's your call.'

She swallowed. It was such a huge step, and she wasn't at all sure she was ready for it, but it would give her baby security, and love, and she would know that if anything happened to her, God forbid, the child wouldn't be alone. And she knew that was something that had worried her mother a great deal.

'If I said yes—there would have to be conditions,' she warned, and he raised a brow.

'Conditions?'

She nodded. 'I want a pre-nuptial agreement, so that my house is protected for the baby. I know that probably seems silly to you, since your house is worth much more than mine, but I need that security, in case anything happens in the future.

And I'm not interested in your house. That's not what this is about. My childhood was so uncertain, and I just want to protect my baby's future.'

She wanted a pre-nup? He nearly laughed out loud. If she'd had the slightest idea how rich he was, just how much family money was behind him, she would have been mortified. But clearly she didn't, or she wouldn't have suggested it for an instant. She'd be mad to.

'Well?'

He smiled slightly. 'OK—but there are conditions on my side, too. At some point, we'll probably end up moving back to Italy. Can you do that? Would you?'

Her eyes widened. 'Move there? To live?'

'*Si*. It's my home. It's where I live, where I want my child brought up, ideally, surrounded by his family, so that he knows who he is and understands my place in his life, but we'll make sure the house will remain cared for so you can stay in it when we come back to England to visit your friends and family, if you don't want to stay in mine.'

'Luca, I can't!'

He lifted a brow. 'Can't? Can't what?'

'Live in Italy,' she said, panic starting to choke her. 'I can't speak a word of Italian, Luca! I struggled to order a coffee.'

'You can learn, *cara,*' he said, his voice softening persuasively. 'It's not so hard. And all my family speak perfect English. Think of the advantages—beautiful countryside, a warm, loving family…'

'Suffocating, you said,' she reminded him, the panic invading every part of her, and he smiled gently.

'They can be, but mostly it's wonderful. And the weather is fantastic. You'll love it.'

He let his words hang for a moment, then lifted his shoulders. 'So that's my choice for us, anyway. I marry you, we live in Italy, at least at some point in the future, and we bring up our child—our children—together. The choice is yours, *cara*. You don't have to marry me, of course you don't, but there are huge advantages for all of us, and I know it'll mean compromises for you, but we can't just think about ourselves any more. Let me know when you've decided—but you need to know that this will be a proper marriage, one that we work on together. I'll give you and our child the protection of my name, but you won't have affairs and neither will I, you and the child will live with me and there will be no divorce, Isabelle. When I marry, it will be for life. I won't betray you, and I'll give it everything I have, but I won't give up on us, and I don't expect you to. So don't say yes unless you're absolutely sure.'

She stared into his eyes, her mind reeling. Live in Italy, with Luca—or here, without him, with the child dragged from pillar to post, shared custody, rows about access, the trauma and drama of holidays and birthdays and Christmas? And in Italy there'd be a family, a great, huge suffocating family to love their baby to pieces.

If she didn't marry him, there was the possibility that she could face the future alone and without support. She had friends and family, but would they pay her bills when she was sick, or look after the baby if she died?

She felt her jaw sag, and snapped it up and turned away hastily. She hadn't given that possibility serious thought, but what if she *did* die? Accidents happened. Would he have her baby? And if so, would he know their child, or would it be a stranger to him? Would the baby know him, if they lived in different countries? Or even be able to speak the same language as its new-found family?

'Difficult, isn't it, *cara?*' he murmured, and she closed her eyes and took a steadying breath. Emotion was another thing, she'd discovered, that pushed her nausea over the edge, and she could feel her throat closing with the prospect of all that uncertainty.

If her mother had been the one to die and not her father, would she have gone to him? And would he have loved her? What if she didn't marry Luca and he married someone else who had his children? Would her child be welcomed by them if she died, any more than she would have been welcomed by her father's other family? She doubted it.

At a time when his or her world had already fallen apart, her baby could be lonely and isolated and afraid. Without any emotional security.

And that, above all, was the thing that mattered. Luca and his family represented security, a safety net for all of them, and that was something she'd never had and always yearned for.

There was no contest, really. She found a rather wobbly smile and took a deep breath.

'Yes,' she said softly. 'I will marry you, Luca. And we'll make it work.'

He closed his eyes briefly, and when he opened them again, he was smiling. 'Thank you. I'll tell my mother—she can start planning.'

'Planning what?' she asked, a horrible suspicion suddenly entering her mind. 'I don't want a big wedding.'

He laughed. 'Neither do I, but I have a huge family.'

'No. I'm not joking, Luca. I won't marry you if it has to be a big wedding. I was going to do that last time, and it was all planned and bought and organised, right down to the name cards for the tables. I don't want that again. I just want to marry you.'

He studied her thoughtfully for a moment, then nodded slowly and to her surprise he backed down. 'OK—but I want to do this surrounded by my close family, at least, and some old friends. And your mother should be with you, *tesoro*. We could get married in the local church?'

She shook her head. 'No. Can't we get married in a registry office? I just—I want a really simple ceremony, no fuss. Just a couple of witnesses. Please, Luca. I can't face all that razzamatazz.'

'We must have family.'

She shrugged. 'Really? It hardly seems worth it—it's not like it's a proper wedding. It'll be over in half an hour.'

Luca opened his mouth, shut it again and said nothing. She was asking him to marry without his family, in a civil ceremony—because it wasn't a *proper wedding?*

'It will be a proper wedding,' he told her firmly. 'It will just be quiet. Please, *cara*. Do this for me. Marry me in Tuscany— we can have a quiet wedding there.'

'Very quiet,' she insisted.

'Of course. Just our families and maybe a few close friends.'

She nodded. 'I'm sorry—I know it's probably not at all what you had in mind.'

'*Tesoro,* none of this is what I had in mind, but it's all negotiable, and if this is what you would like, then it's what we'll have. We can have a civil wedding in the town hall followed by a church blessing and a small reception. OK?'

'Won't your mother mind?'

He laughed softly. 'It's not up to my mother. It's our

wedding, we'll have what we want. I won't tell them yet, though. I'll save it until we get there. And now I'm going to leave you to rest. I'll see you tomorrow.'

He stood up, drew her into his arms and kissed her tenderly, then wrapped her firmly against his chest. 'Just a few more weeks, *cara,*' he murmured, and eased away from her, kissing her fleetingly once more before letting himself out of the house and closing the door, leaving her alone to wonder what on earth she'd talked herself into.

'You're doing *what?*'

'Going to Italy with Luca to meet his family, and to plan our wedding.'

'Ohmigod, you jammy thing!' Sarah exclaimed, her eyes filling. 'Oh, that's fantastic!'

Was it? Fantastic, to be planning a wedding when she was pregnant with his child?

Yes, actually, she realised, it was—not that Sarah knew about that, because they'd agreed not to tell anyone yet, but the baby was getting more real with every hour that passed, and Luca was spoiling her rotten. She still wouldn't yield on the clothes, though, and so she enlisted Sarah's help. 'I need your advice. I'm going to need lots more clothes for when I go to meet them, and I want decent ones, but I won't let him buy them for me.'

'You must be mad. I'd let him. Hell, any man that wants to take me shopping can have me. The only place I get to go these days with a man is the supermarket, and that's only to make sure I buy him enough meat! For heaven's sake, Izzie, he's going to be your husband!'

'Shh!' Isabelle chuckled and shook her head. 'Not too

loud, we're not broadcasting it. Anyway, I'm not letting him do it, so what can I do on a shoestring?'

'Charity shops. I know just the one,' Sarah said, her eyes alight. 'There's a woman who brings the most gorgeous things in, and they're too tall and too tight for me, but they'd fit you perfectly, and they're fabulous. Some of them still have tags on. We'll go tomorrow.'

So they did, and by a stroke of luck they arrived just a few minutes after another consignment from the mystery lady.

And they were a perfect fit. Half an hour later, Isabelle emerged with three dresses, four tops, a jacket, another pair of trousers—and there were even a pair of Jimmy Choos in her size that looked unworn, and the prices were ridiculous. Even so, she'd still spent part of her re-roofing budget, but not nearly as much as if she'd gone to the designers directly—and the charity would benefit, which was an added bonus.

'Oh, you're so lucky, I love those shoes,' Sarah said wistfully. 'Oh, you're going to look fabulous.'

'I hope so. I really don't want to let him down.'

'Don't be absurd! How on earth could you let him down? Who the hell *is* he? Anyway, you're wonderful. He should consider himself lucky to have you.'

Isabelle didn't bother to explain. She wasn't sure she really knew, anyway, and she just hoped that yesterday's fashion would be good enough.

He was waiting on her doorstep when she arrived home with a carrier bag in each hand emblazoned with the name of the charity.

'Where have you been?' he asked curiously.

'Shopping,' she said, cursing her luck that he should have been there so she couldn't smuggle the things into her house without him knowing.

He frowned at the bags. 'In a charity shop?'

'Why not? If I'm having to buy clothes for Italy, I can't afford to do everything in the high street shops,' she said, aware of how distinctly frugal she was being with the truth, but he just frowned.

'You went to a charity shop for clothes to wear to meet my family?' he said, looking appalled, and she met his eyes defiantly.

'It's called recycling. Very environmentally sound.' And cheaper by miles.

'But I offered—'

'I know. And I declined. Besides, it's pointless spending a fortune because they won't fit me for long, and I hate waste. Do you have a problem with that?'

His mouth opened, then snapped shut. 'No. No problem,' he said through clenched teeth, and she suppressed a smile.

'Good. Just so we both know where we stand. Don't worry, it's all really good stuff, I won't disgrace you.'

'I didn't think you would for a moment.'

'Good. What's in your shopping bag?'

'Food. Some of it could do with going in the freezer. Luckily it's not warm out here.'

She felt a pang of guilt and quickly suppressed it. She hadn't been expecting him, hadn't asked him to shop for her, and it was in no way her fault that he was there mid-way through the afternoon. Then she remembered he'd been on call last night and this was his afternoon off, and then she did feel guilty, because he was probably exhausted.

'You should have rung me.'

'I did. You weren't answering your phone.'

Just then it let out a series of beeps, and she pulled it out and found several messages about missed calls from him. 'Sorry. I must have been on the Tube. Come on in. I'll put the kettle on.'

'I'll do it. Go and hang up your things.'

He went into the kitchen, inwardly seething, and listened to her pottering upstairs with her charity shop finds—charity shop, of all things!—while he put the shopping away and made them tea, dropping the tea bag in the bin just as she ran back downstairs.

'Perfect timing. Here—it's ginger and lemon.'

'Thanks. So—have you had a nice afternoon?' she asked brightly.

'Busy. I've booked the flights for Friday morning. We need to be at the airport at six-thirty. I take it your passport's valid?'

She nodded numbly.

'Good. We're going via Pisa because my car's in Firenze. I'll get it delivered to the airport ready for us.'

She caught her jaw in time. Get it delivered? It was slowly beginning to dawn on her what she was getting herself into, and she felt a shiver of apprehension. Maybe she should have let him take her to Harrods—or not.

This way, at least, her pride would be intact, and she was reasonably confident she wouldn't disgrace him, but— Friday? Dear heaven.

CHAPTER SEVEN

THEY TOUCHED DOWN late in the morning on a gloriously sunny day, and Isabelle was never more glad to be back on land in her life.

Her legs were wobbly, her heart was pounding and she'd struggled with nausea for the entire flight. And now they were standing outside the airport in the brilliant early March sunshine, and all she wanted was to go somewhere still and quiet and lie down for a while until the vibrations had gone from her body and her heart had slowed.

Not that that was likely to happen in a hurry. She was on a knife-edge, filled with apprehension over meeting Luca's family, no matter how wonderful and welcoming and marvellous he said they were.

'Come on, let's get you home,' he said, and she nearly laughed hysterically. Home? Her safe, cosy little house in Herne Hill with its shabby décor and tired furniture that she couldn't afford to update, with its roof in need of attention and its tiny courtyard garden filled with pots that she would plant up later in the year—that was home.

'*Isabella?* Are you all right, *cara?*'

'I'll be fine.'

'We'll take the main road, it's quicker. They're expecting us for a late lunch.'

Her stomach turned over at the thought, but she didn't know if it was lunch or the family which worried her more. She fell into step beside him as he towed the luggage across to the short-stay car park and unlocked his car—the outrageously sexy Italian sports job she'd last been in when he'd brought her here all those weeks before, after the night that had changed both their lives forever.

'So how did you get your car here?' she asked, still amazed by that ridiculous detail and trying to focus on something other than the upcoming meeting.

'I had it dropped off by the garage where I store it if I'm out of the country,' he said, and stashed their cases in the boot before settling her into the seat. The leather was warm, and she relaxed back against it with a little sigh.

'All right, *cara?*'

'I will be. The turbulence was a bit much.'

There had hardly been any, he thought, but she'd looked doggedly out of the window for the entire journey, her face chalk white, and he wondered if it had been the turbulence or if she was just nervous. Not that she normally seemed a nervous person. Rather the opposite, but he guessed there was a lot going on today and he already knew she wasn't a good flyer. Still, the flight was over now, and there was only the drive left. With a quick glance into his mirror, he pulled out into the traffic and set off for home.

His parents were expecting them, but he hadn't told them anything about Isabelle because he didn't want them making a great fuss and putting on some massive welcoming committee that would scare her off. He was just happy that she was here, that he'd got her here at all. She was tense enough as it was without any added fuss.

He put his hand on her leg and gave it a quick squeeze, and she glanced across at him and smiled fleetingly.

It was all she could manage. Her stomach was in knots, and the nearer they got to his home, the worse it became. Thank God the main A1 Rome road was smooth, although it twisted and turned and plunged from time to time into long, dark tunnels as it wove through the Tuscan hills.

Then they turned off onto the twisting little minor road that wriggled its way through the beautiful rolling countryside, the picture-postcard landscape of Tuscany unfolding in front of her, with the avenues of cypress trees like sentries along the roads, the little hilltop towns sprinkled along the way keeping guard against the Florentine invasion.

'It's beautiful,' she said softly, staring out at the scene so familiar from postcards and paintings that it was almost a cliché now, and yet in the flesh she found she loved it, and the tension started to leave her, taking the nausea with it.

'It's my favourite place in the world,' he told her. 'And not just because it's home. It's also very beautiful in a stark, rather severe way, but there are problems here, of course, which the tourists don't see. It's hard to keep the young people here in the old towns. There's nothing for them. Agriculture is dependent on the weather, and not everyone wants to make wine or olive oil or cheese, or act as a guide for the tourists. So they go to the cities—to Siena, to Firenze, to Pisa—or further, maybe, to Roma or Milano, and so the elderly lose their support and the schools lack children.'

'But your family are still here, and you keep coming back.'

'We belong here,' he said simply, and with a sudden shock

she realised it was true, that this was his home, and if she'd imagined that when they got married she could talk him into living a cosy little life in London away from his family, she was almost certainly deluded.

And beautiful though the landscape was, she couldn't imagine it feeling like home, and she wasn't sure how she felt about that.

He decided to go straight to the lodge so she could rest and freshen up before going to meet the family, but when he turned onto the drive he could see cars over there clustered in front of the building. Several cars—or vans. Workmen?

Damn. That meant it was out of action, and of course the alternative to being in the lodge was to be in his usual room in the house, with her in the adjoining room. Damn. At least in the lodge they'd have had a bit more privacy, which was why he'd suggested it, and he much preferred the simplicity of the lodge.

Not that the privacy was an issue, and maybe it would be easier in the house to maintain a little more distance. It had been an unwritten rule that whatever any of them did, they would be discreet and not subject the family to their romantic entanglements until they were married. And so far, only Massimo and his sister Carla had tied the knot. The rest of them—Gio, Anna and Serena—were still single. And him, of course, at the moment. But not for much longer.

Beside him, Isabelle sat up a little straighter. 'Are we nearly there?'

'Yes, but we can't stay at the lodge. There are vans outside—it must be being decorated or something.'

She turned her head towards him. 'So where will we stay?'

'In my parents' house.'

She looked ahead along the curving drive lined by an avenue of trademark cypress trees, but the only buildings she could see were a village in the distance and a huge stone edifice, more like a castle than a house. A fortress? Or a fortified hill town, but so small it only had this gravel road to it? That was what it looked like. A little fortified hill town. But of course his parents' house was also a farm, so perhaps that was the house and the farm buildings and all the offices and workers' accommodation. That would make sense.

And maybe it would be smaller close up. She'd find out soon enough, she told herself as they drove along the gravel track and up the hill.

'Massimo will be here—he runs the family business and lives here with his children. He's a single parent—he lost his wife shortly after their third child was born—she had a brain haemorrhage.'

'Oh, how dreadful! How old are the children?'

'Eight, five and three, or something like that. I don't know. They grow up so fast. They live in a wing of the house.'

A wing? So maybe it wouldn't be smaller...

'Gio's here, too,' he said, as they went through a great archway into an area at the front of the huge building and pulled up beside a black Ferrari. 'I thought he might come to check you out. Come on. Let's go in.'

She opened the door and got out, transfixed by the size of the building. So much for her idea that it might be smaller than it appeared. It was truly huge, even larger close up, great sweeping steps climbing to the huge double doors on the first floor, and as she stared at the forbidding and impressive entrance, the door opened and an elderly man hobbled down the steps towards them, holding out his hands in welcome.

'Signore!' he cried, and she realised in shock that this man must be the archetypal ancient retainer, and this enormous edifice, this monumental building, was Luca's family home.

Luca turned towards him with a smile and took his out-stretched hands, touched as ever by the warmth of the old man's greeting.

'Roberto! It's good to see you again. How are you?'

'I am well, *Signore*. And you?'

'Very well, thank you. Is my mother inside?'

'Si, Signore. And your father. They're expecting you, and your brothers are with them. Carlotta said to tell you lunch will keep until you're ready.'

'Good. Thank you.' He switched to English for Isabelle's benefit. 'Roberto, let me introduce you to a friend of mine, Isabelle Thompson. She'll be a guest with us for a few days.'

Roberto's eyes swivelled to her, standing very still a little behind Luca, and he hauled himself up straighter and beamed a welcome. *'Signorina,'* he said gravely, bowing low, 'Welcome to the Palazzo Valtieri.' And then he turned back to Luca, and embraced him. 'It's good to see you again,' he said, reverting to Italian. 'You've been gone too long. Carlotta is very excited. She's busy cooking for you.'

Luca laughed softly. 'Thank you.'

'Now I will take your luggage upstairs.'

'No. I'll do it. I'll take Isabelle up and let her change and freshen up, and then we'll go and meet my parents. Just tell Carlotta we're here—oh, and get some Prosecco on ice. We have something to celebrate.'

'Si, Signore. At once!' And he scurried off, shaking his head and grinning from ear to ear.

'Right. Let's go and find my parents,' he said.

'Do you supply maps?' she asked a little drily, and he gave a tired laugh.

'It's not that big.'

'Not? Luca, don't be ridiculous! It's enormous!' Isabelle exclaimed, still reeling. 'I mean, I knew it would be big, but this is crazy! Why didn't you tell me?'

'Because it's nothing to do with anything.'

She rolled her eyes and glared at him. 'Luca, you have *servants!* You live in a *palazzo,* for heaven's sake! That is not *nothing!*'

She climbed the first few steps, staring around her and taking it all in, her heart pounding.

It was stunning. Absolutely stunning. Huge terracotta pots containing what looked like olive trees flanked the broad steps which led to the massive dark wooden doors in the centre of the house, and tall windows were arranged symmetrically in three rows across the front, taking advantage of the spectacular view. At roof level, high up over the front door, was what looked like a massive mantel clock with a fine black iron frame above it supporting a brass bell.

And then she thought of her little house that he'd been so damning about, and the pre-nuptial agreement she'd asked him to sign before their marriage, and she wanted to die of humiliation.

She didn't feel so much out of her depth as nailed to the bottom of the ocean, and she was furious with him for not warning her. Or with herself for not having worked it out. She felt so ill prepared, so stupid, so totally unready for this whole meeting that she could have wept.

But she wouldn't. She was made of sterner stuff than that. Instead she tucked her bag under her arm and went down to the back of the car where Luca had removed the cases from the boot. Thank God for Sarah and her charity shop, she thought, and reached for her case, only to receive a warning growl.

'I'll take that. You're not carrying anything except the baby,' he said firmly, and she gave in. Let him carry it, if it made him feel good. She didn't have the energy to argue. Instead she straightened her shoulders and followed him up the steps and through the great heavy entrance doors.

She wasn't going to cry, and she wasn't going to waste her energy arguing. She was busy saving it for the coming confrontation, when his parents met her and realised that their son had brought home a plain, very ordinary and slightly pregnant Englishwoman for their inspection.

Oh, well. Look on the bright side. At least the baby didn't show yet...

'They'll be in the salon overlooking the garden,' he told her. 'Would you like to take a shower and change into something fresh before we go and join them?'

She was staring around her at the frescoed walls of the colonnaded logia around the central courtyard as he led her through the villa to the main stairs, and she looked utterly overawed. 'Please,' she said quietly, and he felt a prickle of guilt for the fact that she'd had to travel when she still wasn't feeling good—but what was he to have done?

Flying at this stage wouldn't hurt her or the baby, and he was keen to introduce her to his family and let her see the home that he loved so much—the home he hoped to return to at some point in the future. And he badly wanted her to love it at least a little.

'Maybe I should let you rest—go and talk to them myself first.'

'Warn them about me, you mean?' she said drily, and he grimaced.

'That's not what I meant.'

'But it's what you'll have to do, Luca. They don't know anything about me, never mind that I'm pregnant—they'll be so upset.'

'No. They'll love you.' *As I do.*

The thought shocked him into immobility for a moment, but she didn't notice. She was busy studying the frescoes on the stairs, her face growing more and more serious.

'These are wonderful, Luca. This must be a really important house.'

He pulled himself together. 'It may have been one of the Medici villas. The provenance is a little uncertain, and it had a chequered history before my ancestors acquired it. It's been in my family for over three hundred years.'

She was silent then until he led her into the bedroom adjoining his, and again she stared around in shock. As well she might, he thought, because in comparison to the frescoed halls, it was almost monastic in its simplicity, and that was the way he liked it.

There were no plastered ceilings in this part of the house, just terracotta tiles between the beams to match the floors, and the walls were white.

But it was the view that held Isabelle's attention, and she stood at the window and stared out over the landscape, her face turned away from him so he couldn't read her expression.

'Is this land all yours?'

'Yes. Pretty much what you can see from here belongs to the family.'

'I thought you were farmers,' she said, her voice shocked, and he winced.

'Well, we are, in a way. Growing grapes and olives is farming.'

She gave a tiny but distinctly unladylike snort. 'How large *is* your farm, Luca?'

He shrugged. 'I don't know. You'll have to ask Massimo, he's the figures man. Several thousand hectares. I'm not sure how it's divided up. About one third each of pasture, vines and olive groves. I'll take you on a guided tour—or get him to do it. He'll be better, if you're really interested. It's his passion.'

She turned away from the window, her nerves starting to get the better of her the more she found out.

'Is there a bathroom? I'd like to wash and change, then we need to go and drop this bombshell on your parents,' she said, and he could tell from her expressionless face how much she was dreading it.

'Sure,' he said, and opened the bathroom door. 'Help yourself.'

She took her washbag from her case and paused in the bathroom doorway.

'You don't need to wait,' she told him. 'I'll come and find you when I'm ready. Where will you be?'

'My bedroom's through that door. We share the bathroom. I'll go and get changed—give me a tap when you're finished so I can shave.'

She nodded and closed the door, turning her back to it and staring round at the very modern and beautiful fittings. Marble walls, a huge walk-in shower with a head the size of a dustbin lid and a bath you could get an entire family in.

She looked at it longingly, but settled instead for a shower, which made her feel a little better, but by the time she'd dried and dressed herself in her new trousers and a soft sweater, her heart was pounding.

She went into the bathroom and tapped on the door. 'I'm finished,' she called, and the knob turned and he came through it.

'Thanks. I won't be long.'

He'd changed his trousers, but he'd taken off his shirt and the sight of that shadowed jaw above his beautifully muscled chest made her mouth dry. She backed away, shut the door to her side and walked to the window, sitting down on the padded window seat and staring out over the beautiful rolling countryside.

A few minutes later he tapped and came through, looking good enough to eat. 'Are you ready?' he asked.

'As I'll ever be,' she said, and stood up, running her hands a little nervously over the front of the trousers. 'Will I do?'

He smiled at her and nodded. 'You look lovely. Cool and fresh and composed.' His smile softened. 'They're just people, *cara*. That's what my old university professor used to say to us about patients, whether they were intimidating or from a very humble background. "We're all just people." Remember that.'

'Just so long as they do,' she murmured under her breath, and squaring her shoulders and lifting her chin, she followed him through the twisting, winding corridors, down the ornately frescoed staircase to the courtyard, and then round to the other side and into a huge room overlooking the terrace.

'Ah, they're outside, taking advantage of the sun.'

A group of people, three men and a woman, were sitting under a beautiful colonnaded pergola entwined with the stems of jasmine, just bursting into leaf, and he took her by the hand and led her towards them, their feet crunching over the gravel and alerting the dogs, who leapt up and ran towards them, tails wagging furiously as they greeted Luca and checked her out.

'Luca! *Figlio mio!*' An elegant middle-aged woman got to her feet and hurried over to him, hugging and kissing him, and then her eyes found Isabelle's and she let him go and put her head on one side, a hesitant smile touching her mouth, as if she was uncertain of her ground. As well she might be, Isabelle thought, suddenly presented with a strange woman on the arm of her son.

'And you must be Isabelle. Welcome to Italy,' his mother said, and she thought there was something a little wary about her eyes. Oh, lord, what am I doing here? she thought, but then his mother smiled and took her hand. 'I'm Elisa, and this is my husband Vittorio.'

'I'm very pleased to meet you. I'm sorry, I don't speak any Italian—I feel really rude but I will try and learn it.'

'It's no problem. We all speak English,' Vittorio said. 'It's good to meet you, too. Welcome.'

He shook her hand firmly, his eyes assessing but less wary than his wife's, and then she was being introduced to two men who were clearly related to both the others—Luca's older brother Massimo, who apparently ran the estate, and his younger brother Gio—the lawyer who'd delivered the thinly veiled threat, owner of the black Ferrari and with a distinctly speculative look in his eyes.

Then Roberto hobbled up with a tray of glasses, and someone appeared with an ice bucket and champagne, and a plump, white-haired woman who looked almost as old as Roberto bustled in with a tray of nibbles and Luca took the tray from her, set it down and swept her up into his arms.

'Carlotta!' he said, kissing her wrinkled cheek, and she laughed and coloured like a girl and said something in Italian.

'*Si.* Carlotta, this is Isabelle. *Cara,* Carlotta knows more about me than anyone in the world. She delivered me, and my father before me, and she is a very important member of the family. She is also the *cucinare*—the cook—and so even more important. Be nice to her.'

She laughed and smacked his hand, then turned to Isabelle with a beaming smile. '*Signorina,*' Carlotta said, taking her hand and clasping it in both of hers, her eyes sparkling with delight. 'Welcome.'

'Thank you.'

She rattled off something in Italian, and Luca laughed and translated.

'Carlotta's a superb cook. She says she's looking forward to cooking for you.'

Oh, lord. And she'd have to eat all sorts. Well, she was feeling a little better this week, so maybe it would be all right.

'*Si.* I look after you,' she said, patting her hand, and for a moment she wondered if Carlotta had realised she was pregnant. No. She couldn't have done. It didn't show.

'*Grazie,*' she said with a smile.

Carlotta beamed and said, '*Prego,*' and waddled away, wheezing slightly.

Prego? she thought in panic, and then remembered it meant something on the lines of 'You're welcome' and was nothing to do with pregnant.

But then she forgot Carlotta, because Luca slid his fingers through hers and held her hand firmly against his side, and said, 'We have something to tell you.'

The family snapped to attention. Luca's fingers tightened

fractionally, and, turning to her, his eyes smiling reassurance, he went on, 'Isabelle has done me the honour of agreeing to become my wife.'

He didn't get any further, because his mother gave a little cry and threw her arms around them both, then his father was moving her gently out of the way so he could kiss Isabelle on both cheeks, his eyes, so like Luca's, warm with welcome.

Then it was Massimo's turn, at first a formal handshake, then a hug and a smile, and it was down to Gio.

Gio, who'd warned her not to hurt his brother, who'd told her she'd have him to deal with and that he never lost in a court of law. He walked over to her, took her hand and bent to brush his lips against her cheek.

'Welcome to the clan, Isabelle—but remember what I said and be kind to him,' he murmured, and stepped back, the smile not really disguising the warning in his eyes.

But Luca was there, his arm round her again, holding her firmly by his side in a demonstration of possessive affection that nobody could misunderstand, and she met Gio's eyes and didn't back down. Why should she? She had no intention of hurting Luca. She just hoped he felt the same way.

'So, we have to plan the wedding!' Elisa said, clapping her hands. 'Oh, Luca, we'll get Anita tomorrow, she'll be marvellous—and, Massimo, call your sisters, tell them to come, we need to celebrate! Vittorio, open the wine!'

'Mama, slow down, we want a quiet wedding,' Luca said, laughing softly. 'A hundred people, max.'

'A hundred!'

Isabelle and Elisa spoke in unison, but she had the feeling her future mother-in-law was appalled at the small number, whereas she—

A loud pop interrupted her thoughts, and Vittorio poured the Prosecco into the glasses. 'Here, *cara,* welcome to the family,' he said kindly, handing her a glass, and she had a tiny sip before Elisa came over to her and took her hand and led her to the chairs.

'Come, sit next to me and tell me all about my new daughter-in-law. I can't tell you how much I've looked forward to this day. I was beginning to wonder if Luca would ever find a woman he could love, but he has. I can see it in his eyes, and I'm so happy for you both.'

She didn't bother to correct her. How could she? But in the warmth of her welcome, she was able to forget about Gio's warning for a while, and concentrate on getting to know her future husband's family.

They moved inside when the wind picked up, sipping wine and nibbling all sorts of tasty little treats until Roberto called them to the table, and while the conversation ebbed and flowed around her, Isabelle watched them all and wondered what it must be like to grow up in a family. Suffocating? She didn't think so…

'See? I told you they'd love you.'

'Well, some of them. Gio's a bit suspicious.'

'Ignore him. My mother thinks you're wonderful.'

'I think your mother's wonderful—a really very nice woman, but she doesn't know about the baby yet,' she pointed out, and stifled a yawn. It had been a long day, starting before six that morning with the drive to the airport, and it was almost nine at night now.

Lunch had gone on until almost four, and they'd had a light supper an hour ago. Now, they were strolling hand in hand along the terrace, snuggled up in coats and letting Carlotta's plain but delicious food settle before they went to bed.

It was nice to be alone, she thought. His family were lovely, but she was tired, and as they stood there in the cool of the evening she yawned again.

'Come, *cara,* you've had a long day. You need to go to bed,' he murmured, letting go of her, and she felt a pang of loss.

They walked back along the terrace, then up the steps to the pergola where they had all sat earlier, and he took her hand again as they went in through the doors into the lovely sitting room. His parents were there, sharing a last cup of coffee before bed, and they looked up and smiled.

'*Buonanotte,*' he murmured, and his mother blew him a kiss.

'Don't hurry in the morning,' she said, a smile in her voice. 'Breakfast can wait for you. You are on holiday now, and you both work too hard. Enjoy it.'

'Thank you,' she murmured. 'Goodnight.'

'*Buonanotte,* Isabella—and welcome.'

As they walked back through the corridors and courtyards, their footsteps echoing quietly in the night, she felt awe again that he lived here, in this spectacular house—that this was his home, his birthright. And it would be her child's.

The thought was daunting.

He opened the bedroom door for her, and she saw that the room had been prepared—the covers turned down, her case emptied and set aside, her clothes presumably hung up in the cupboard. More evidence, as if she needed it, of the gulf between them.

Her nightdress and dressing gown were laid over one side of the bed, and she turned to him in the doorway. 'What time do you want me to get up tomorrow?' she asked, and he shrugged.

'I don't. Please yourself—I'll be around. Give me a call on my mobile when you wake up and I'll get you something light to eat before you get up—and come and ask me if you need anything in the night. I'm going to find my brothers now and have a drink with them, but I won't be long. Call me if you need anything.'

Only you, she thought as he bent his head and kissed her. And then he was gone, the door closing softly behind him, leaving her alone with her tumbling thoughts and emotions.

'So what's the story, then?'

Luca dropped into the battered old leather sofa in Massimo's apartment in the house and rolled his eyes.

'Gio, shut up,' Massimo said softly. 'Luca, what can I get you? I've got a nice Pinot Grigio in the fridge, or there's a lovely Barosa open.'

'No, I've drunk enough.'

'Rubbish. Give him the Barosa, loosen his tongue a bit. I want to hear all about his *bella regazza*. I can see why you've fallen for her. She's gorgeous. I just hope it hasn't blinded you.'

'Leave her alone, Gio. She's done nothing to deserve this treatment from you.'

Gio arched a brow. 'Let's just wait and see.'

'Shut up, Gio. Where did you meet her?' Massimo asked, butting in.

'Firenze, in a café, in January.'

Massimo put a glass in his hand. 'The day of your interview? You dropped off the radar for twenty-four hours. Could this be anything to do with the lady in question?'

He gave a soft snort and nodded. '*Dio*, does nothing escape you guys? Yes. I spent the day with her.'

'And the night,' Gio prodded, and he sighed.

'Do you have to be so damn rude?'

'That's a yes, Massimo, by the way. So how come you're working with her?'

'It's just coincidence.'

'Yeah, right.'

'No, really. I'm helping a friend out with a locum job—'

'Why? You're right in the middle of your research paper,' Massimo said, getting to the heart of it. 'And what happened about the professorship in Firenze?'

'I took a rain check.'

'To follow her back to London,' Gio said, and Luca realised they were going to drag every last painful millimetre of this out of him.

'Yes, if you must know,' he confessed, to get it over with. 'I wanted to find her. And I couldn't. So I took a job with Richard, and there she was.'

'She seems a little wary,' Massimo commented, swirling his wine thoughtfully in the glass.

Luca snorted. 'Wouldn't you be? You were watching her like hawks, especially Gio.'

'Mama seems to have taken to her new daughter-in-law, anyway. Does she realise she's pregnant, I wonder?'

'Is she?' Massimo asked, looking shocked, and not for the first time that night Luca felt the urge to kill his little brother.

The silence seemed to stretch on and on, and finally he cracked and broke it. 'Yes. Yes, she is. The baby's due in September.'

He met Massimo's eyes, and after a second his brother sighed softly.

'Oh, hell, Luca. Are you OK with it? I take it she really is pregnant?'

'Yes, she really is.'

'Don't sound so indignant. It wouldn't have been the first mistake of that sort.'

Luca cut Gio a slashing look. 'I'm an obstetrician. I think I can tell by now when a woman's pregnant,' he said cuttingly.

'Oh, I don't doubt she's pregnant,' Gio said. 'But are you sure it's yours?'

'Yes,' he said tightly.

'Why?'

'Because—there are sound reasons why that I have no intention of going into with you, and I have no reason to doubt her, because I trust her,' he told them bluntly, ignoring Gio's snort of disbelief. 'As for how I am about it, that rather depends on whether you guys put her off completely before the wedding. That's why we're here—so she can learn all about me from you, and see if she feels she can trust me. We don't exactly know much about each other, but we need to. I thought this would fast-forward it a bit, but I'm relying on you.'

Gio swore softly, and Luca waited for the mockery that would follow, but there was none. Not this time.

'What do you want us to tell her?'

'That I'm not a lying, cheating bastard like her father and her ex-fiancé would be good.'

Massimo winced. 'Ouch. So it's not just you with a messy past, then. OK. Consider it done.'

He looked at Gio, who shrugged. 'OK. But I'll be watching her.'

'I never doubted it for a moment. There is one thing you'll like, though. She wants a pre-nup.'

'What?' Gio started to laugh, then shook his head in disbelief when he realised Luca was serious. 'Why?'

'She has a house—a two-bedroomed terraced house in Herne Hill. She wants it protected for the baby if anything happens to us.'

'Is that likely? I know what you feel about marriage.'

'No. No, it's not likely, but it's what she wants, so she can have it.'

Gio gave a low laugh. 'Does the woman have any idea what you're worth?'

'No—well, she didn't, not until we got here. And I thought there was something very touching about the way she wanted to protect the baby if anything went wrong.'

'Or could it be the fact that she doesn't trust you?'

'She's been hurt. Trust is hard. Anyway, my money's irrelevant. It's not who I am, Gio.'

'On the contrary, Luca. It's very much who you are, and who you are is too damn trusting. I'll make sure your interests as well as hers are protected. I'll draw you something up in the morning.'

'She gets half,' he said firmly. 'And I want a will, not a prenup. The other half goes to the baby.'

Gio went pale. 'Hell, Luca. Massimo, give him another drink. He's lost his mind.'

'No. I think, actually, he might just have found it,' Massimo said with an understanding smile, and topped up his glass.

The following day was a whirlwind.

Massimo was going to take them round the estate in his car after he'd dropped his children at school, but at the last minute something cropped up, so he lent them the off-road car and they set off as soon as they were ready.

'I'm sorry about his wife. He's a really nice man,' Isabelle said to Luca as they drove away.

'It was dreadful. I don't think he'll ever marry again. He adored her. They were childhood sweethearts. He's a nice guy. A good friend. He likes you.'

'Gio doesn't.'

'He doesn't trust you. He's got his reasons—it's not personal.'

'The woman who hurt you ten years ago? Tell me about it, Luca. What happened?' she said, but he wouldn't go into it, and then they arrived at the winery for their guided tour with the manager, and the opportunity was gone.

The rest of the morning was taken up by their tour of the estate—even larger than she'd imagined—then lunch in a trattoria some miles away before the return journey through the arable part of the land. 'That's Anita's family home over there, on the top of that hill,' Luca said as they paused on a rise. 'She's an old friend, more of a sister really, and she's a wedding planner. We'll talk to her later. No doubt Mama will be discussing things with her already. She's dying to meet you.'

Was she? Really? 'How good a friend?' she asked, and Luca shot her a wry smile.

'Not that good. I tried—she slapped my face when I was sixteen, and I haven't dared to try again. She's very nice. You'll like her.'

She hoped so. A wedding planner? It sounded a bit scary, but she needn't have worried. Anita *was* lovely, and hugged her warmly when they met at the end of the afternoon, after their tour was over.

Then, once the introductions were out of the way, she shooed Luca and his mother away and settled down in the corner of a comfy sofa with a glass of fruit juice on the table

beside her, tucked her feet under her bottom and produced a
notebook from her bag. 'I like to talk to the bride on her own,'
she said with a grin. 'Everybody has so many opinions, but
really only one person's opinion matters. So, talk to me.'

'About what?' she asked, at a loss. 'I haven't really thought
about it—not the detail. I've done all this before—got right to
the wire,' she admitted reluctantly, because she wanted Anita
on her side. 'Then it all went wrong and it never happened. So
I don't want anything remotely like what I'd planned before,
because apart from anything else, none of it was my choice.'

'OK, so tell me about your dream wedding for you and
Luca,' Anita said.

'Oh. Well, we're not planning my dream wedding, are we?
Just something quick and quiet. I've got over the dream scenario.'

Anita tutted. 'You should never get over your dream
wedding.'

'You do, believe me, when you see how easily it all turns
into a nightmare.'

'So how was it, while it was still a dream in your head,
when you were a little girl? Tell me about your dress—what
did you want? Tulle? Satin? Lace?'

'Raw silk. I never really knew what it was, and I'm still
not sure I do, but it sounds so lovely!'

Anita laughed. 'I agree. So—silk?'

'I think so. But ivory, I think. White's a bit harsh against
my skin.'

'Ivory suits most people better. Or maybe even a pale dove
grey, or soft coffee?'

'Coffee might be nice.'

'And what about the style?'

Isabelle shrugged, not sure quite how to deal with this one, so in her usual way, she met it head-on. 'I don't know. When I was a child, I always wanted to be a princess, but most princesses aren't pregnant when they get married.'

Anita's eyes widened, and she clapped her hand over her mouth and gasped. 'You're having a baby?'

She nodded, wondering why Anita was so shocked. And if it was anything to do with Gio's hostility. Had Luca had a baby in his past? Was that it?

'It's due in September, so I'd like to get married soon, before it shows. Another eight weeks, maximum. And we don't want a huge do.'

'But—it's your wedding! Luca's family—'

'Will do as they're told,' Luca said, coming into the room with a tray of tea and cakes. 'Here, something to keep you going while you plan. I'm going for a walk with Papa, I'll see you later. Nita, don't bully her.' And stooping down to Isabelle, he kissed her lingeringly on the lips, winked at Anita and walked out.

Anita shook her head, staring after him with a thoughtful expression. 'He'll be a wonderful father. He's brilliant with children. Have you met Massimo's tribe yet?'

She shook her head. 'No, not yet. They'd gone to school when I got up.'

'They're lovely. They adore their Uncle Luca. So, while I pour the tea, tell me all about your fairytale princess wedding…'

CHAPTER EIGHT

THE WEDDING WAS scheduled for the last Sunday in April—ludicrously quick compared to those of her friends who'd married recently. Their weddings had taken at least a year to plan and cost about half a year's salary or more.

Not hers. Apart from the fact that they simply didn't *have* a year to spend planning it if it was to happen before the baby was born, they didn't have any planning to do. Anita was doing it all, after asking Isabelle all sorts of questions that she couldn't believe were actually relevant to such a small wedding.

'Leave it to me to sort out the details,' Anita said with a smile after the date was set. 'Just talk, and I'll make sure you have the day you want.'

She wasn't sure it was in Anita's control to give her that, because the thing she'd want at the top of her list was a husband who had chosen her for herself and not for the fact that she was pregnant. And no matter what he might say, there was no way she'd ever know the truth about that, so she put it out of her mind and concentrated on getting through the days.

Their holiday was wonderful, his family were lovely and once he'd told them there was a baby on the way they pulled out all the stops to sort out the wedding as quickly as possible.

There were dress fittings—dresses in all sorts of subtle off-whites and coffee-creams, some spangled with crystals, others delicately scattered with pearls or tiny beads. Strapless, off the shoulder, high necked, halter—the choice was bewildering, but they narrowed it down to a simple dress in raw silk with a sweetheart neckline, pleats fanning from the waist on one side and a little duster train, in a delicate coffee cream sprinkled lightly with pearls. And a veil, even though she protested that it was hardly appropriate, but Anita shook her head and told her that it was a family heirloom and it would mean breaking with tradition to marry without it.

'It's probably breaking with tradition to be pregnant,' she said drily, but Elisa blushed and shook her head, so with a little laugh Isabelle agreed to the veil.

And then they were back in London, where they'd be working right up until the week before the wedding.

She was still feeling nauseous, despite Luca's intervention every morning with apple slices and dry toast and his constant nagging all day to eat little and often, tempting her with little tasty snacks. He'd moved her into his house as soon as they'd got back from Italy which slashed her journey time almost to zero, insisted she change her work pattern to something less taxing and he cooked every evening unless he was on call. Without him she had to admit she would have really been struggling.

And every night, he went into his bedroom beside hers, closed the door and kept severely to himself.

'I don't want it to change the way we feel, and if we sleep together now, it will. I don't want to cloud the issue, *cara*,' he told her. 'And I want you to feel free to change your mind right up to the last minute. I would rather you did if you weren't still absolutely sure.'

But she was more sure than ever with every day that passed. Working with him was fascinating, challenging and a source of constant debate and discussion, but in the evenings after work was over, after they'd eaten and before he sent her up to bed before him, they would sit side by side on one of the soft leather sofas and wrangle over the television remote, or he'd lean over and give her the word she was groping for in a crossword or wait for her to go to the loo and correct the mistake in her Sudoku which was holding her up.

And if she challenged him about it, he'd just grin and say nothing.

It was surprisingly easy to live with him, she was learning, and gradually her fears for their future were ebbing away. His reaction to her scan had been interesting, too. He must have seen hundreds—no, thousands—but not, of course, of his own baby, and he'd taken her hand and hung on tight, his eyes riveted to the screen as the tiny little heart had blipped away, and his eyes had been over-bright. And after that, he'd taken to touching her there, over the baby, his hand gentle, his eyes smiling.

They were lying in front of the television one evening, his hand idly resting on her tummy as his fingers caressed the tiny curve that was the only very slight evidence of her baby, when he said out of the blue, 'Have you thought about the birth?'

'Mmm. Of course.' She'd thought about little else, wondering what it would have in store, and knowing that so long as Luca was beside her, it would be all right. 'I think I'd like a water birth. I've got a lady scheduled for one just before we go away—Naomi. She's got a cervical suture—she's already lost two babies, the first at twenty-four weeks, the second at twenty-one. She has an incompetent cervix and they've been devastated, but she's been all right this time. She had the suture in nice and early, and we're hoping for a natural labour. She should be an ideal candidate, and I can't wait. I've told her to call me and I'll go in whatever, even if I'm not on. I really want to be with her.'

'Not that you're getting too involved,' he teased, and she laughed.

'Well, I am, and this time I've got a personal interest. I really want to do another water birth and it should be a good one. I have a feeling it'll be quick, so you'll just have to take the suture out nice and promptly first thing in the morning so she's delivered by the end of the day to make sure I can be there. And I'll just hang on until she has it.'

'You don't need to. You'll only be here—unless we're in Italy.'

She shook her head. 'She won't go that long. I have a feeling about her. I bet you she's admitted before the suture's scheduled to be removed.'

Luca groaned. 'Your feelings are all too accurate for my liking. Just tell me when she's there.'

'Are you busy, Isabelle?'

'No—do you need me?'

He nodded. 'There's a new admission just arriving. She's specifically asking for you. If you wouldn't mind?'

'Sure,' she said, only too grateful to get out of the staffroom before Sarah started quizzing her any more about the wedding.

'So who's this woman?' she asked, and Luca smiled wryly.

'Naomi Brown.'

'Naomi! Oh, Luca, no! She's not due yet! She's only—what—thirty-three weeks now?'

'Thirty-four and a half.'

'So why's she come in?'

'She's having contractions. We have to remove the suture.'

Isabelle felt a shiver of apprehension. 'Oh, lord. Luca, we have to make sure they keep this baby. They were devastated when they lost the others. We have to save it for them.'

He stopped and turned to her, and his smile was crooked. *Cara,* I fully intend to save this baby whatever the mother's history, and at over thirty-four weeks, that shouldn't be an issue. Come on, let's go and see her. If her labour's not yet established, perhaps we can delay it.'

'And if not? Are you happy for her to have a water birth still, because she really wants it, Luca.'

'Probably. Let's go and see if we can stall it first.'

But they couldn't. Her cervix was fighting against the suture, and as soon as Luca had removed it, Naomi's distress eased and she sighed with relief.

'Oh, that feels so much better,' she murmured. 'Thank you.'

'My pleasure,' Luca said with a smile, getting up off the stool and moving out of the way so they could reinstate the end of the bed. 'Now we'll just keep an eye on things and see how you go. It may be fairly fast, your cervix is already thinning.'

Thinning was the understatement of the century, Isabelle thought as she examined her a short while later, the moment the huge delivery bath was filled. Her contractions were coming thick and fast, and she was starting to get distressed again.

'Do you want to go in the water?' Isabelle asked her gently, and she nodded.

'Please. I know this is a bit hurried, but—you know, we planned it, Isabelle, and I'd love to do it. I just think it's so gentle for the baby.'

'It is, for both of you. Come on, we'll get you in now. It's all ready.'

She and Ryan, Naomi's husband, steadied her as she stepped into the warm bath, and as she sank down into the welcoming water she gave a sigh of relief.

'Oh, that feels so good. Can we turn the lights down?'

'Sure.' Isabelle lowered the lights, Ryan turned on some soft instrumental music and Naomi rested her head back, moaning softly from time to time, but utterly relaxed as Ryan knelt beside her outside the pool and stroked her tummy slowly.

Then she opened her eyes and looked into Isabelle's, calm and composed. 'I want to push.'

'OK. Let me check you.' She knelt down and leant over into the water and examined her, and not surprisingly her cervix was fully effaced. 'Whenever you're ready,' she said quietly.

She heard the door open almost silently, and knew it was Luca, but she didn't look up, just held Naomi's hand as she pushed. He read her mind, though, because very slowly, so as not to startle them, he turned the lights back up so she could see what was happening.

'OK, the baby's head is crowning now, I can see lots and lots of hair. Well done. Keep going, keep pushing gently. And again. Good girl. You're nearly there.'

Another contraction gripped her, and the baby's head slipped free, followed by the rest of his body in a slithering rush.

'Oh!' Naomi breathed, reaching down to her baby, her face filled with wonder.

'Lift him up out of the water now, nice and gently—that's it,' she murmured, and as Naomi lifted the baby to her breast, he drew in a little breath and sighed.

'Is it all right? Why isn't she crying?' Naomi asked, panicking, but Isabelle just smiled.

'They often don't with a water birth, because it's so gentle. It's fine—he's breathing properly and pinking up nicely. Well done.'

Ryan sucked in a great shuddering breath, and Naomi sagged back, tears pouring down her face.

'Is she really all right?'

'He—you've got a little boy, Naomi—and he's beautiful. Congratulations.'

'Oh, Ryan! We've got a boy—a baby boy!' she sobbed, cradling him tenderly against her. 'Oh, he's so small!'

'He is small, but he's strong. We need to keep him warm,' Luca said, and covered him with a towel, tucking it in round him to protect him from draughts until the paediatric team arrived to take over.

Isabelle blinked away her tears and looked up at him as he straightened, and mouthed, 'Thank you.'

He gave a crooked smile. 'Any time,' he murmured, and as he turned his head away, she thought she saw a tear glisten on his cheek.

A man of his experience, moved to tears by a simple delivery? Except of course it wasn't simple, it was the end of years of hope and grief and heartache for this couple, culminating in the successful delivery of a live baby who would have every chance of survival.

And only a robot would fail to be moved by that.

But nevertheless…

Luca left them to it and walked out, once he was sure the mother was fine in Isabelle's hands and the baby was doing well. He was to be taken up to SCBU as a precaution, and he would have steroids to mature his lungs. There'd been no time to start Naomi on them because of the speed of her labour but, at thirty-four weeks plus, Luca was confident the baby would be fine, and so would the parents, who had gone through so much to reach this point and were now celebrating tearfully.

And Luca, who didn't even know the family, was getting carried along by the sentiment in a way he never usually did. Oh, he loved a successful outcome, and he took pride in the fact that he really cared about his patients, but he couldn't remember the last time a delivery had brought real, wholesale tears to his eyes.

He blinked hard and went into the kitchen to make himself a drink. Not coffee, still, in deference to Isabelle. In fact he was almost tempted to tip the jar into the bin. And then he thought about his own baby, growing slowly inside her, the woman who had changed the course of his life completely. He'd seen her face at the twelve-week scan just after they'd come back from Italy, and he knew that she already loved it.

And so did he.

It didn't surprise him that he felt strongly. What did surprise him was *how* strongly he felt, and he wondered how he'd feel if anything happened to it.

Gutted, he realised. Absolutely, completely gutted. Most of all for Isabelle, but also for himself. It must be worse for the mother, so close to the baby, but the thought of losing it was shocking.

He just hoped everything went smoothly, starting with the wedding. He wondered briefly what he would do if Isabelle changed her mind and refused to marry him after all, but dismissed the negative thought. She wouldn't do that.

Would she?

Well, he'd soon find out. Three more weeks to go. Only two weeks until they flew back to Italy, and three weeks to the wedding, and another twenty-four to the baby's birth.

He realised he could hardly wait.

They flew back to Italy the week before the wedding, and this time she hadn't argued about buying clothes.

Luca had taken her to a boutique in London, and she'd been dressed and undressed a hundred times while he'd sat there and made all the right noises. The price tags were eye watering, but she didn't argue, she just refused to have too many. 'I'll outgrow them in weeks, Luca,' she pointed out. 'We can get something over there if necessary.'

'Of course, but you'll need things for this week.'

'Won't these do? I'm tired,' she protested, and it wasn't really a lie, but she felt guilty about so much wanton extravagance. After all, it wasn't as if he wanted to spoil her. He was doing it out of necessity, but all she really wanted was a few things to wear—and a ring. An engagement ring, a symbol of his love—but of course, although they were getting on well now, he *didn't* love her, and with the wedding coming up so fast, it hardly seemed worth bothering with anything other than a wedding ring.

And Luca hadn't mentioned it.

He was talking to the sales assistant now as she dressed. 'Could you wrap them please and have them delivered to this address?' he said, and as she came out of the changing room he was putting his wallet away, and he turned to her with a smile.

'Lunch?'

Curiously deflated suddenly, she shook her head. 'No, I don't think so. Can we just go home?'

'Of course.'

The following day while she was sorting out their washing ready for Italy, the clothes arrived. Plus some others she'd turned down, and it made her want to cry. It all seemed so unnecessary, she thought, but she packed them anyway.

Two days later, they flew to Tuscany, amid a hail of good wishes from their colleagues and friends at the hospital and promises to throw them a party when they got back.

They arrived at the *palazzo* in the early afternoon, to be greeted with a frenzy of activity.

'Heavens, what on earth is going on?' she asked Luca, but he just gave her a wry smile.

'There's going to be a wedding—remember?'

'But only a small one.'

He snorted, and she felt a wave of panic. 'Luca, you promised!'

'It will be small,' he assured her. 'That doesn't necessarily mean it will be low key. Anita will have organised it all—don't worry. It looks like a lot of fuss, but when they all go away, it'll be just us. Trust me, *cara*. It will be a lovely day.'

Could she trust him? There seemed to be an army of vans and trucks, and when they went through the house to the salon overlooking the terrace, she could see why. The terrace was smothered in white canvas, and as they watched it was hauled upright.

'Good grief! I've never seen a marquee that size!' she said, stunned, and he laughed.

'Come on, let's go and find the family. They'll be in the library, I suspect, overseeing operations from the control centre.'

It sounded terrifying, and clearly everything she'd said had been ignored. It was just like last time, everything taken away from her, planned to death by others to give them the day they were expecting.

But she'd reckoned without Anita.

As they went into the library, she got to her feet and came over and hugged her. 'Hi. How are you?'

'Worried. That marquee's huge.'

'Oh, no, it's a very moderate one. Don't worry. It's for afterwards—the wedding feast is set up at one end, and the dancing will be at the other, and that way we don't have to move the tables. There are more people coming for the evening, as well, but you can slip away then and leave them to it. I expect you'll be tired anyway, and I should think Luca will want you to himself.'

Luca would. Luca wanted her to himself now, and he could see the worry on her face and wanted to take her away from it all, but there was no way they could have got married without a certain amount of fuss, and he trusted Anita.

'Right. We need to freshen up and have some lunch, and then we'll come and see you. No doubt you've got lots of questions.'

'No, not really. Luca, you need a suit fitting this afternoon, and, Isabelle, the designer is here with your dress. She's going to do the first fitting today and then another tomorrow, if necessary, to give them time. I'm sorry to land it on you when you've just arrived, but she'll wait until you've rested.'

'I hope it fits,' she said softly to Luca as they walked up to their rooms. 'I really have no idea if it will, but lots of my things don't now.'

'It doesn't show yet to the casual eye.'

'But there won't be a casual eye, will there?' she said drily. 'They'll all be watching me like hawks, and something like that will be top of their list, with the speed of the wedding.'

'Does that bother you?' he asked. 'Because it doesn't bother me, in the least. I'm not ashamed that you're carrying my child, Isabelle—quite the opposite, and I'm more than proud to show you off.'

His softly spoken words brought a lump to her throat, and with a sigh he opened her bedroom door, took her in and drew her into his arms. 'Hush, *tesoro*. It will be all right. They'll all love you.'

Do you, though? Luca, tell me—!

'Right, I'm going to have a quick shower and go and sort this suit out. I suggest you rest for a while, then come down when you're ready.'

The next few days were a whirlwind of activity, but very little of it seemed to involve Isabelle, and she had little to do but fret.

The guests had started to arrive—his sisters, Carla with her husband Roberto and their three children, and Anna and Serena, unmarried but both with boyfriends in tow, and of course Giovanni, who finally seemed to have decided that she was all right. Massimo of course was already there with his children, and then there was Luca's grandparents too, who'd she'd already met, adding to the numbers, but the result of the influx was that every meal was a feast.

'I'm really not going to be able to get into the dress if I keep on like this,' she said to Anita, who chuckled and told her not to be silly.

'You'll worry it all off—I can see it in your face. Have faith in me, Isabelle. It will be a beautiful day.'

'You have a hotline to the weatherman?' she said with a smile, and Anita laughed.

'Of course! All part of the service. But the long-range forecast is superb. It's going to be a fabulous day.'

'I hope so,' she murmured, but the weather was the least of her worries, and the man who was to become her husband was so involved with his family that she had hardly had any time with him for the last couple of days, and she missed him. Missed working with him, missed spending the evenings alone with him, missed all of it.

She went out onto the terrace and found a seat tucked away in a quiet spot, and then she saw Luca down below her, walking along a path towards his brother Massimo. They greeted each other, and she watched them, her heart wistful. Massimo had loved his wife deeply, and she'd been torn from him, but at least they'd shared that love while she was alive.

She loved Luca desperately, but she couldn't tell him, unless she was sure he loved her too.

'Luca?'

'Hi, Massimo. How are you doing?'

'OK.'

Luca searched his brother's face, and saw sadness in his eyes. 'I'm sorry, this must be hard for you.'

'Don't worry about it. I have something for you.' And he slipped his hand into his pocket and pulled out a little box.

Luca felt a lump in his throat. 'No, Massimo.'

'Yes. Please. I'll never give it to another woman, and she hasn't got a ring.'

'I didn't think of it,' he said, shocked at his lapse. 'I've been more concerned about her and the baby—the ring didn't seem—I've ordered a wedding ring set with diamonds, it's here somewhere, Anita said it arrived today, but—I didn't think—damn. Massimo, I can't take Angelina's ring.'

'Of course you can. It's no use to her, and, anyway, it's a family ring. It belongs in the family, and Isabelle is family now. According to Anita it's even the right size. Please—take it. It should be worn, and I'd be overjoyed to see it on your wife's hand.'

'Oh, hell…'

He took the little box, slipped it into his pocket and hugged his brother hard. 'Thank you.'

'My pleasure.' He stepped back, his face stiff with emotion, and with a brisk nod he walked away. Luca watched him go, then pulled the box from his pocket and stared down at the ring. Would Isabelle accept it from him?

He slipped it back into his pocket, strode up the steps and found her sitting on a seat in the gloom, looking out over the valley.

'Are you all right?'

'Yes. I was watching the swallows. They're amazing—there's a sort of shift change, have you noticed? Just before nine, when the swallows go to bed and the bats come out. It's incredible. Fascinating. I could watch them for hours. And the lights are really pretty. I've been watching them come on in all the little villages. It's beautiful—peaceful.'

'It is peaceful. That's why I love it so much.'

He sat down beside her and took her hand. 'Isabelle, I have something for you. I don't know whether you'll want to accept it, but I hope you will, because it would mean a great deal to all of us.' He hesitated, then went on, 'It's been passed down in the family for generations, and I hadn't even thought of it, because it was Angelina's—Massimo's wife's—but he's just given it to me to give to you, and I know it's a bit late, and the wedding's happening anyway, and it's not what either of us had planned, but—'

He broke off, put his hand in his pocket and knelt down on the gravel in front of her. 'Isabelle, I love you. You once said that loving me wasn't the problem, it was trusting me. And I don't want you to marry me on Sunday unless you feel you can trust me. So—will you marry me? Will you wear this ring for me, to show the world that you love me, too, and that you trust me with your heart?'

Her eyes filled, and she pressed her fingers to her lips and held back a tiny sob. 'Oh, Luca—I never thought I'd hear you say that. Of course I'll marry you.'

'But can you trust me?'

'Yes,' she said, and then, realising she hadn't even thought about it for days, maybe weeks, she said it again, more firmly this time. 'Yes, Luca, I trust you—and I'm so sorry it's taken me so long.'

'Don't be sorry. I've had trust issues, too. The girl in my past—she told me she was pregnant, and I asked her to marry me, doing the decent thing, of course, and then three weeks before the wedding I found out she was on the Pill, and she had been all along.'

'Oh, no—so when I told you I was pregnant…'

'I knew you were. You were very obviously pregnant. But my faith had been shaken, and I wasn't absolutely sure it was mine. But she only wanted me for my money, and when you asked for a pre-nup to protect our baby, I knew then that the baby was ours. Apart from anything else, you didn't know anything about me, so if you wanted me, it was for myself and not for my money. But you didn't.'

'Oh, I did, Luca. I did—but I was so afraid of being hurt, and I knew that if you walked away, it would hurt me so much more than I'd been hurt before, and I'd have to see you over and over again for the next twenty or so years as our child grew up, and it would tear me apart. But you aren't going to walk away, are you? You're not that sort of man, and I realise that now. And I'd be honoured to wear your ring.'

He let his breath out on a sigh, and, opening the box, he took the ring out and slipped it onto her finger.

'Oh, Luca, it's beautiful,' she said, and felt her eyes fill with tears. 'Poor Angelina—will Massimo be all right with this?'

'He said so. He said he'd be overjoyed to see it on my wife's hand.'

He stood up and drew her up into his arms. 'I love you— *te amo, Isabella,*' he murmured, and then he kissed her, his lips gentle on hers. Then he drew reluctantly away with a ragged sigh. 'Only three more days,' he said, and, threading his fingers through hers, he led her up to her room, kissed her again and then walked away.

CHAPTER NINE

THE DAY OF the wedding dawned bright and clear, just as Anita had promised, and Isabelle couldn't wait.

Her mother had arrived two days before with her husband, and she'd been stunned at Luca's family's obvious wealth. Stunned and wary, but the moment she met Luca, she was smitten. 'He's lovely—such a nice man, darling,' she'd said, misty-eyed. 'I'm so happy for you. He's just exactly right for you.'

'I think so,' Isabella had replied, and now, on the morning of her wedding, she just wanted all the hoopla to be over so she could be with him, but of course there was so much to do.

The hair, the nails, the dress, the make-up, the veil—and then finally it was time to go, and she walked down the beautiful stone staircase to the central courtyard with its exquisite frescoes, and Luca, looking more handsome than she'd ever seen him, was standing there waiting.

Luca, who she loved with all her heart.

Luca who, if the expression on his face was anything to go by, loved her every bit as much. He took her hands in his and stared wordlessly down at her, his heart in his eyes, and then, tucking her hand into the crook of his arm, he led her out to the beautiful vintage car smothered in ribbons and flowers, and they set off together for the little hill town nearby.

They were cheered along the way by the estate workers, the villagers and then all the townspeople, and she felt near to tears. 'They really love you,' she said, and he just smiled and waved back.

'They love a wedding. Italians are all deeply romantic.'

'Except Gio.'

'Oh, he's romantic. He's just disillusioned. I was the same, but then I met you, and everything changed. Wave to them, *cara*. This is as much for you as it is for me.'

They pulled up outside the town hall, and amongst the cheers she heard the word *'bellissima'*. Beautiful. Her? Her eyes filled, and she smiled at them, and they cheered again.

The town hall, when they managed to get inside, was packed. 'I thought it was going to be small?' she murmured spotting her friend Sarah and Richard Crossland in the crowd, and he laughed softly and squeezed her hand.

'This is small,' he assured her, and then paused, staring deep into her eyes. 'Last chance to change your mind,' he murmured.

'No,' she said firmly. 'I love you, Luca. *Te amo.* Let's get married.'

It was nearly midnight before they got away.

They'd been wined and dined, there had been speeches, and everything had been punctuated by cries of 'Kiss, Kiss!' and Luca, laughing, had dutifully kissed her, again and again and again, until by the time they'd been dancing for a while she could feel the tension radiating off him.

Then another cry went up, and he stopped dancing, cupped her face in his hands and plundered her mouth with his, while everyone cheered and catcalled all around them. Then he lifted his head, his eyes glittering, scooped her up in his arms and carried her inside in a hail of confetti and sugared almonds.

'Where are we going?'

'To our new quarters. We've got the two big rooms on the end overlooking the terrace.'

'Two rooms?'

He gave a lazy, sexy smile. 'Only one bedroom. The other one's a sitting room.'

'They'll see the lights,' she said as he carried her in and turned them on, and he laughed.

'They know what we're doing, *tesoro*,' he murmured. 'It's not a secret. Does it worry you?'

She thought of all the people outside, people she'd never met, but others whom she'd grown to love, and she shook her head. 'No. I'm not ashamed to be in love with you. I'm proud to be your wife, Luca, and it's been a very long wait. But you could close the curtains.'

They slept late the next day—and the day after, and the day after that.

After all the hustle of the wedding, it was wonderful to relax and do nothing, and now, in the middle of her pregnancy, Isabelle felt really well.

They went sightseeing around some of the little hill towns, and walked through the pretty streets while he told her the history of each one, and they walked through the forests and sat under olive trees in the shade and ate impromptu picnics of bread and cheese and ham with ripe, juicy tomatoes which dribbled down their chins, and then they had to kiss the juice away, of course, so that on most days they came home early and went back to bed, using her pregnancy as an excuse, but nobody believed them and neither of them cared.

They were deeply in love, blissfully happy, and life was wonderful.

And then at the end of the week, he took her to a friend's private clinic for her routine twenty-week scan to check for problems, and it all fell apart.

'Are you sure about the dates?'

'Absolutely,' she said. 'It could only have been one occasion. Why?'

'Because the baby seems a little small. I would say it was eighteen, maybe nineteen weeks from the skull measurements.'

Beside her, Luca went very still, and Isabelle felt her heart start to pound as she began to flick the pages of a mental midwifery textbook. 'Is there anything else?' he asked, and his friend shrugged.

'Not that I can see. It's hard—the baby's position isn't the best, I can't get a good view of the heart, but the spine's OK and the skull's a good shape. It's not anencephalic, if that's what you're thinking, and the placenta looks OK.'

'The heart,' Luca said. 'Why can't you get a good view?'

'It's a bit shadowed. I don't know. We'll have to give it two weeks and check again, to see if we can get a better look and to make sure the baby's growing, but I think the most likely thing is that you've got the wrong dates.'

'But we can't. We haven't.' She was feeling sick, fear for her baby beginning to swamp her, and she reached for Luca's hand, but it wasn't there. He was standing staring at the screen, his hands rammed deep in his pockets, and he didn't say a word.

'Luca?'

'We'll come back,' he said, and helped her wipe the gel off her tummy with curious detachment. 'Two weeks?'

His friend nodded. 'That should be long enough. I'm sure it's nothing to worry about.'

Maybe not for him, but for them it was going to be an eternity, Isabelle thought as she sat in the car beside a silent Luca all the way back to his home.

'Luca, why?' she asked, worrying. 'What can it be?'

'There's no sense speculating,' he said, and so she sat there and speculated and worried and panicked on her own, while he maintained a stony silence.

They pulled up at the bottom of the steps, and he helped her out of the car and in through the door. 'Go and rest. I've got things to do,' he said, and disappeared without another word.

'Luca?'

But he didn't hear her, because she'd only mouthed the word, and she stared after him, a horrible suspicion dawning.

Surely he didn't believe that the dates were wrong, did he? Because that would mean that he thought the baby wasn't his.

'No!'

She bit her lip, and then, turning away from the cloistered courtyard, she ran upstairs to their room and threw herself sobbing down on the bed. He couldn't believe that! After all they'd been through, the journey they'd made to reach this point of trust, to have it all wiped away so easily was devastating.

So devastating, in fact, that the only thing she could think of was getting away. She didn't even care about her luggage. Her own clothes, ones bought with her own money, were at home—her real home, the one her mother had struggled for so many years to buy. Her mother was there now. She'd go home to her, go and see Richard Crossland and ask him what could be wrong with her baby, and then she'd deal with whatever fate threw at her alone.

Her passport was in her handbag, and her mobile phone. She'd learned enough Italian to get herself to the airport. All she needed was a lift down the drive—and Roberto would take her.

But, first, she needed to see Massimo.

She found him in the office at the back of the house, and he got to his feet with a startled exclamation when he saw her.

'Isabelle, *cara,* whatever's wrong? You look dreadful— come, sit down, what is it?'

She shook her head, and with shaking fingers she tried to pull the ring from her finger—the ring he had given Luca to give her barely a week ago—but it wouldn't come off, and she started to cry again, and he pulled her gently into his arms and hugged her while she wept. 'Oh, Isabelle, no—what is it? Talk to me.'

'I had my scan—and there's something wrong, the baby's small, and Luca doesn't believe me now—he thinks it isn't his.'

'No. No, I don't believe that. He was so sure, he had such trust in you.'

'Well, not any more. He thinks I've lied, and I haven't, there must be something wrong with my baby, and I can't bear it, Massimo. I can't bear it if anything happens to my baby.'

'Hush, *cara,* hush, this is wrong. Let me ring him.'

'No! I just wanted to give you this back, and I'm leaving.'

'No!'

'Yes. I can't stay. I have to get away— Here.' She tugged it off, scraping her finger and making it bleed, and she dropped it in his hand and turned away, heading blindly for the door and a life without another man who'd let her down…

* * *

He thought he'd felt pain before, but it was nothing compared to this, this pain like a knife through his heart.

He'd gone over and over it, but there were so many things it could be, and none of them were good. The heart? *Dio,* not that, he thought, his mind searching the vast number of things that could cause a baby to fail to grow.

And he'd let her fly—let her work ludicrous hours, when he should have told her to sit at home with her feet up and rest—should have brought her back here right at the beginning and made her take it easy instead of working fifteen hours at a time and then flying back and forth.

He jackknifed out of the chair and strode out onto the terrace, but the sun was too bright and his mood was too black. And then he saw her, a distant figure stumbling down the drive, hurrying away.

'No!'

His phone rang, but he ignored it and ran for the car, just as Massimo came out. 'Luca! Isabelle's gone.'

'I know! Why didn't you stop her?' he raged, but he didn't wait for the answer, just threw himself into the car and shot off down the drive after her, his heart in his mouth. What the hell was she doing in the full heat of the sun, running along the uneven road? And why?

He skidded to a halt just in front of her and leapt out, running back and grabbing her arms. He just stopped himself from shaking her, but he wanted to, to shake some sense into her.

'What are you doing?'

She jerked herself upright and glared at him, her face ravaged with tears. 'I'm leaving. What does it look like?'

'But why?'

'Because you don't believe me. Because you think I've lied to you about the baby being yours.'

'No! *Tesoro,* no! Never!'

'Then why wouldn't you talk to me?' she screamed, tears coursing down her dusty cheeks and leaving muddy trails in their wake. She scrubbed them away, biting her lip and fighting for control, and he felt another crushing wave of guilt.

'Oh, Isabelle, my love—I couldn't talk,' he said unsteadily. 'I was going through all the things it could be, wondering what was wrong with our child, if it would live or die—'

His voice cracked, and he let go of her and turned away, his shoulders heaving, and she stared at him, taking in his words, letting them sink in and make some sense of this sad and senseless day, and then tentatively she reached out her hand and laid it on his shoulder.

'Luca? Please hold me.'

He turned, his face contorted, and dragged her hard up against him, and together they stood on the long, winding drive and wept.

Finally he lifted his head and led her into the shade of a cypress tree, and they sat down side by side, his arm around her shoulders, and he spoke softly to her, her hand wrapped firmly in his.

'I was so busy blaming myself and feeling guilty for letting you work so hard and making you fly, and not letting you have your quiet little wedding, and all the time you thought I didn't believe it was mine? Oh, Isabelle, I thought we'd got past this.'

'I thought we had. I thought you would have talked to me, shared your fears.'

'I wanted to protect you from it.'

'How?' she asked. 'By refusing to discuss it? I'm a mid-wife, Luca—I know all the things it could be. How did you think not talking it through would help me?'

He shook his head. 'I'm sorry. Of course it wouldn't, but I was afraid to put too much into your head. I should have realised it was already there from the first suspicion that everything wasn't right. I'm so sorry. I can't believe you were running away.'

'I thought you didn't trust me. I couldn't bear that.'

'I'm sorry. Of course I trust you. You're far too honest to lie about a thing like that. That's one of the things I love most about you.'

He pressed a gentle kiss to her forehead, and she leant against him with a sigh, taking comfort from him and at the same time offering it.

'Luca, what are we going to do?'

'Wait,' he said quietly. 'What else can we do? We wait, and when we have the next scan, we'll hopefully have more answers.'

'And if there's something wrong? I mean, there might not be. It could just be a little baby. I was working too hard, and I should have stopped, and I wasn't eating properly, and I was so busy being stubborn I didn't do the best thing for the baby, but what if—'

'Hush,' he murmured, pulling her closer. 'It's not your fault, and working hard and flying and the wedding are not responsible. If we're logical, we both know that, but we're doing what people do when things go wrong and blaming something or someone instead of just accepting fate. And if there *is* something wrong,' he said, 'then we'll face it together, and somehow we'll find the strength to do that, and to work through it together and support each other and our child.

Whatever it is, however great or small, we can deal with it, *cara*. It *will* be all right. Come on, let's go home.'

And getting to his feet, he held out his hand to her and pulled her up beside him. Then he saw her hand and lifted it questioningly, frowning at the little scrape on her finger where her nails had scratched it.

'Where's your ring?'

'I gave it back to Massimo,' she told him, and he tutted and smiled gently.

'Then we'll go and get it, and put it back where it belongs,' he said, and putting his arm round her shoulders, he steered her carefully back to the car.

The next two weeks were agony, but they spent them together, for the most part. On the last day, though, he disappeared, and she found him eventually in the little chapel at the side of the house, sitting quietly.

'Luca?'

He looked up and smiled, and held out his arm and she snuggled under it, glad to have found him.

'I lit a candle for our baby,' he said. 'I do it every day. It's funny, I haven't prayed for years, but I've prayed more these last two weeks than I have in my life.'

'Asking for miracles?' she asked, moved by his simple words but unsure about the power of even that much prayer, and he laughed softly.

'No. Not miracles. Just strength, for both of us.'

'It's nice in here—tranquil. It reminds me of your house in London in a way.'

'Do you want to go back there?'

'Why?'

He shrugged. 'I don't know. I just wondered. If there is something wrong, then I'd like to come home, really. The family would give us so much support, but I don't want you to be unhappy, and I know you have reservations.'

'Not any more,' she said truthfully. 'They've been so wonderful the past two weeks—well, all the time, really, but especially recently—and I've grown to love it here. London was always my home, but only because it was where I lived. But this—this could be home, too, in a different way. But you'll have to help me with my Italian, and I'd like my mother to come often—will you help with the air fares, Luca?'

'Of course. Don't be absurd, they can come as often as you like. And maybe we'll need a house of our own.'

He left his thoughts hanging, but she could read his mind, and only the scan would answer that question. If then.

He looked at his watch. 'It's time. Shall we go?'

'Well, there's the heart—and it looks good. The flow's excellent, the vessels all look fine—and the baby's grown. Have you been resting?'

She laughed a little, and squeezed Luca's hand. 'Yes, I've been resting,' she told him.

'Well, it must have just had a slow start, because it's caught up now—I would say it's just a few days behind, maybe three or four, and that could be simply that it's a small baby—a girl, probably, but I'm not sure without looking. Do you want to know?'

'No.'

They spoke in unison, and Luca went on, 'It doesn't matter. All we have to do now is sit back and wait. Oh, and find a job here in Tuscany, at some point, before I forget how to deliver babies.'

His friend laughed. 'How about the professorship? It's still up for grabs.'

'Professorship?' Isabelle said, stunned, and he gave a wry grin.

'Mmm—in Firenze. That was the job I turned down.'

'For me?' she said, even more stunned. 'You turned down a professorship *for me?*'

'*Si*. Because I loved you—from the first moment I saw you through the café window.'

'Oh, Luca,' she said, and started to laugh, but the laughter turned to tears of joy and relief, and as he gathered her up into his arms, his friend went quietly out and closed the door behind him...

EPILOGUE

ISABELLE STRAIGHTENED UP and arched her back, exhausted.

Heavens, the house had been dirty, she thought, and then the backache grew and spread, and she rested her hand over the baby and felt the contraction ease.

She glanced at her watch, and went into the kitchen to make a drink. It was probably just a Braxton-Hicks, she'd been having lots of them.

'Ahh!'

She sagged against the worktop, hanging on and staring out over the valley at the Palazzo in the distance. It was mid-September, and they were harvesting the wheat, and Elisa was visiting Carla and the children, snatching the chance before Luca's baby arrived.

She was alone, and she was having contractions every three minutes. That wasn't good.

She went into out onto the veranda of the old shooting lodge and uncovered the birthing pool again. She'd just scrubbed it out and rinsed it thoroughly in preparation— because she'd known? Maybe.

She turned on the taps, all plumbed in in readiness, and started to fill it. It had to be at exactly the right temperature, thirty-seven degrees, and as it filled she would need to adjust it to keep it right.

Well, it would give her something to think about till Luca got home, she thought, and then another contraction took her breath away. The moment it was past, she phoned the hospital and said, in halting Italian, 'Could you please page Professor Valtieri and tell him his wife's in labour and he's needed at home? Yes, that's right. Now, please. Thank you.'

Then she put the phone down within reach, turned on a soothing CD, peeled off her clothes and stepped into the water. Bliss. The music soothed her, the water was perfect, and the next contraction washed over her.

She tuned into it, feeling the power of it sweep through her body, and as she rested her head back, she relaxed her muscles and allowed them to do their work.

'She's *what?*'

'In labour—I'm sorry, *Dottore,* I tried to page you but they said you were in Theatre, and I had to find you to tell you…'

His secretary's words faded into the distance as he sprinted for his office to grab his car keys and phone. As he headed for the car park, he stabbed the speed dial for Isabelle and fumed impatiently until she answered.

'Are you all right?'

'I'm fine. I'm in the pool.'

'Who's with you?'

'No one, but I'm fine, Luca. I'm propped up, I can't slip, I'm really comfortable and don't even contemplate suggesting I get out. Just get home carefully.'

'I'm on my way,' he said. 'Ring me—any change, ring me. How close are your contractions?'

'Two minutes.'

He swore, fluently and succinctly, and gunned the car out of the car park into the stream of traffic heading out of the city. He hit the A1 in record time, drove faster than was sensible but slower than he wanted to, and skidded onto the drive a little over an hour later.

'Isabelle!'

He ran out to the veranda and found her lying in the water, panting softly, her eyes closed and her legs drawn up. And he could see that the baby's head was crowning.

Dear God.

He tore off his shirt, knelt down beside her and kissed her gently on the shoulder. 'I'm here, *tesoro.* I've got you.'

'Mmm,' she sighed, and then made a little pushing noise and the baby's head was delivered. She put her hand down and stroked it, and a smile drifted over her face, and he felt a huge lump in his throat. He'd so nearly missed this.

'You're doing really well,' he murmured, holding her, and then with the next contraction, their baby was born and she lifted it, silent and peaceful, up to her breast.

He reached out, blinking away the tears, and laid his hand on the soft, soft skin of his child. It was pale, as babies born underwater so often were, and as it took its first shuddering little breath, its face went pink, then its body, then its arms and legs.

'Hello, baby,' she murmured, turning it so it could reach her nipple, and he got his first clear look at his baby.

'She's a girl,' he said, his voice cracking. 'She's a girl, Isabella. She's beautiful.'

'Can you check her? Please? Make sure everything's all right?'

'*Si.*' He took his tiny daughter from her, his hands sure and confident, and wrapped her in a towel. It wasn't cold—the weather was beautiful—but he didn't want her to be chilled. He dealt with the cord, then laid her down on the towel beside Isabelle's pool so she could watch and he checked her thoroughly.

Eyes, nose, mouth, ears, head, neck, hands, fingers, feet, toes, hips, bottom—perfect. And indignant now, wanting her mum, angry at being disturbed when she'd been so peaceful, and he smiled and lifted her to his shoulder.

'Hush, baby. I need to look after your mama. You rest now.'

And putting her down in the waiting crib and wrapping her up gently, he turned back to his wife.

'That was amazing. I'm so glad I was able to have a water birth, it was just wonderful.'

'I can't believe you did it without me—if I'd been any later—'

'Shh,' she said, smiling at her frowning, panicking husband. 'You weren't, so it's all right, but maybe next time you'd better book a good chunk of time off and be a little closer.'

'Next time?' he said, smiling quizzically, and she smiled back, then looked down at their little daughter, asleep at her breast.

'Oh, yes. And the time after, and the time after that.'

He laughed, then hugged her. 'How can you even talk about it so soon? Crazy woman.'

'Crazy about you,' she murmured, and his smile faded as a dozen emotions chased across his familiar and beloved features.

'Oh, *tesoro.*' He closed his eyes briefly, and when he opened them, they were bright with tears. 'I love you,' he said gruffly. 'You and our beautiful little daughter. I can't believe how much light and joy you've brought into my life.'

Unbearably moved, she reached up a gentle hand and cradled his cheek. 'I feel the same. My life was empty without you, Luca, and now I've got so much—you, our daughter, your family—but most of all, you. I love you. *Te amo,* Luca.'

'Te amo, Isabella,' he murmured, and, bending his head, he touched his lips to hers in a kiss filled with tenderness and promise—the promise of a future rich with warmth and love and laughter, fiery with passion and with a deep, enduring trust to underlie it all.

He would be there for her, his kiss said; so long as there was breath in his body, he would be there for her, as she would for him. Forever…

MEDICAL™

Single titles coming next month

A SPECIAL KIND OF FAMILY
by Marion Lennox

When Dr Erin Carmody crashes her car and is
rescued by GP Dom Spencer, the intense attraction
between them knocks her sideways! As Erin begins
to heal, she realises that she belongs with
this handsome single father and his boys. But will
Dom ever trust that their love is truly real…?

EMERGENCY: WIFE LOST AND FOUND
by Carol Marinelli

Every doctor dreads recognising someone in Casualty,
so when James Morrell has to treat his unconscious
ex-wife Lorna, he's shocked! As she recovers, James
realises he doesn't want Lorna as his patient – he
wants her as his wife, this time forever!

2 FREE

BOOKS AND A SURPRISE GIFT!

We would like to take this opportunity to thank you for reading this Mills & Boon® book by offering you the chance to take TWO more specially selected titles from the Medical™ series absolutely FREE! We're also making this offer to introduce you to the benefits of the Mills & Boon® Book Club™—

- ★ **FREE home delivery**
- ★ **FREE gifts and competitions**
- ★ **FREE monthly Newsletter**
- ★ **Exclusive Mills & Boon Book Club offers**
- ★ **Books available before they're in the shops**

Accepting these FREE books and gift places you under no obligation to buy, you may cancel at any time, even after receiving your free shipment. Simply complete your details below and return the entire page to the address below. You don't even need a stamp!

YES! Please send me 2 free Medical books and a surprise gift. I understand that unless you hear from me, I will receive 4 superb new titles every month for just £2.99 each, postage and packing free. I am under no obligation to purchase any books and may cancel my subscription at any time. The free books and gift will be mine to keep in any case.

M9ZED

Ms/Mrs/Miss/Mr ....Initials ....
BLOCK CAPITALS PLEASE

Surname ....

Address ....

....

....Postcode..............................

Send this whole page to:
UK: FREEPOST CN81, Croydon, CR9 3WZ